CLEANED OUT

SUZANNE WILLIAMS

PADDISON PRESS

Cover designed by Shay Stewart

Printed in the United States of America

First Printing, 2022
ISBN 979-8-9869653-1-4
Paddison Press
www.paddisonpress.com

To Dave, who encouraged me to see this through each time I suggested giving up. And to Natalie, who helped make this story the best it could be.

ONE

I gripped the straps of my backpack with sweaty palms. My mind told me I was ready for this, but the rest of my body disagreed. My heartbeat quickened and my stomach clenched. I stood facing the sprawling, stone building that was East Point Prep, slowly working up the courage to walk inside as if I truly belonged. This was it. This was going to be my year. I just had to repeat it until I truly believed it.

It had been almost three months since I set foot inside this building, and absolutely nothing had changed in that time, but confidence was just a mindset, right? I was done with the shy and lonesome cleaning girl persona. I might not have been rich. I might not have had a car or even a driver's license, and I might not have been in any clubs or on any sports teams, but I still deserved my place at East Point, and it was time to start acting like it.

I walked toward the front entrance behind a group of boys. One with a mop of curly hair that covered his eyes held the door for me, even though I was several paces behind him. I started to hurry, not wanting to keep him waiting too long, but then slowed myself. Scrambling to get to a door didn't show poise. It showed nervousness, and the new Darcy was not nervous. At least, not outwardly. I casually entered through the open door. "Thank you," I said.

"You're welcome," he said, swinging his head back to adjust the hair in his eyes.

I smiled and continued up the main staircase to the second floor, where a majority of the eleventh-grade classrooms were. My homeroom was down the hall to the right. Many of the seats were still vacant, but I chose a spot in the back of the room out of habit. I only had one friend at East Point Prep, and I knew I wouldn't see her until lunch, which meant I wasn't going to talk to anyone right away. It's best to look occupied in situations like this, so I took out my phone and opened up Instagram. It wasn't a surprise that I didn't have any notifications or unread messages. I hadn't posted much over the summer, and rarely interacted with anyone on the app, but I still enjoyed the mindless scrolling, and the fact that being on my phone helped me hide how eager I was to see who else was going to be in this room with me.

The best thing about sitting in the back was all the people-watching opportunities. After a few minutes, I noticed Matt Holmes and two of his friends, Tristan Ivanov and Jordan

Schneider, sit down a couple of rows up on the left. Matt Holmes was hot by most standards. He was tall, with strong shoulders and a chiseled jawline. Of all the boys in the junior class, he was the one who looked most like a man in his uniform tie and blazer. He had been playing varsity football since our freshman year, but never came across as the typical jock. Although I had never had a conversation with him, I could tell he had a sensitive and intellectual side. In English class the year before, he'd read an excerpt of his essay on *The Awakening* expressing genuine empathy for Edna Pontellier. He brought up the fact that marriage was often used to trap women, and that he hoped no one in our generation would experience marriage that way, which made my heart nearly explode. After that, my crush on Matt Holmes was undeniable, but I knew with ninety-nine percent certainty that I would never have a chance with him. After all, we hadn't spoken a word to each other in two years, even though we'd been in many of the same classes. Whether it was because he didn't notice me or didn't like me, I wasn't sure. I wasn't sure if he even knew my name. And besides, he had been dating Paige Evans since practically the first day of high school.

I watched as Matt and his friends settled into their seats, wondering if they might glance in my direction. Of course, they didn't, so I went back to my phone, desperately trying not to stare at the back of Matt Holmes' head. I looked up again when I heard the sound of someone writing on the chalkboard. Mr. Maloof, the homeroom teacher, was writing *Welcome Back* in big, swirly letters. The school day would officially start in one minute, and it was then that Paige Evans came into the room with her best friend Audrey. But instead of sitting next to Matt, who had an empty chair beside him, she went clear to the other side of the room, barely even looking his way. Matt looked at her with a pained expression on his face, but then looked away quickly, his friends sneering in Paige's direction. Clearly, something about their relationship had changed over the summer, and I needed to know what it was.

...

"You have to clean today?" asked Maya, opening a bag of pretzels.

"You know it." I unpacked my garlic hummus and carrot sticks. We sat at a table in the far-left corner of the cafeteria. In the middle of the cafeteria were the 'popular' ones, where the athletes and student council executives sat. The further away you were from the middle, the less popular you were. That seemed to be the general rule every year, although how or why it had become so well established, I didn't know. It was just something we all understood, and Maya and I understood our place in the furthest possible corner.

"Ugh, but it's the first day of school. Doesn't it take at least a week for things to get dirty?" asked Maya. "That's going to make your breath stink, by the way."

"I'm not planning on making out with anybody today, so it's fine. And you'd be surprised by how fast this place can turn into a dump if it doesn't get cleaned daily."

Maya had been my best and only friend since freshman year. We were both the poor kids at East Point Prep, something that bonded us as we sat together in homeroom, gawking at the luxuries that it seemed everyone but us had—brand new iPhones, designer shoes and handbags, Range Rovers and Bentleys. But aside from our lack of expensive swag, our situations were different. She was the second of four kids, and I was an only child. Maya's parents, who were still married, worked together in a small restaurant chain that they owned (so they aren't really poor, just not as mega-rich as everyone else at the school). I, on the other hand, was raised by a single mom who had to move in with her parents after giving birth to me so that she could quit her bartending job and finish her nursing degree.

The only reason I was at East Point Prep was because the principal, Mrs. Masterson, was married to the attending physician who worked at the ER with Mom. When Mom realized that the schools in our neighborhood weren't going to cut it academically, she asked Dr. Toth if there was any kind of scholarship his wife could offer us. She even brought him her tax records and my report cards from the previous two years. A week later, he informed her that Mrs. Masterson had already awarded the only scholarships for the following year, but that she'd just had a janitor resign. So, Mom called her up and made an arrangement. I would stay after school to clean every day, and she would give us heavily discounted tuition in return. It might not have been fun, or beneficial to my social life, but it was the only way I was able to attend East Point, for better or worse.

"I was thinking of joining the Debate Team," said Maya. "Their first meeting is today. I wish you could go with me."

"You know I can't do clubs. I'm too introverted to be on the debate team anyway."

"I know," she said with a sigh. "I just need to find more extracurriculars before I start filling out my college apps. Drama alone might not be enough. And I hate going to these club meetings by myself."

"Maybe it would be good for you to be seen without me once in a while," I said. "You know being my friend makes you a reject by association."

"Not true," she snapped, throwing a pretzel at my face. "I don't want to be friends with these rich-ass snobs anyway."

Maya had always been loyal to me, but I knew she didn't mean what she said—not completely. Maya was a social butterfly at heart. She could always make small talk with the popular kids in between periods or while changing for gym in the locker room. She never really solidified any lasting friendships with them, but sometimes I thought she would have if she hadn't always been hanging around me. But I tried to remember my new outlook about happiness being a mindset. Maybe the same went for popularity. Maybe if I just pretended to be popular, more friends would naturally come my way. The problem was, I had no idea how to do that.

"Speaking of rich-ass snobs, I'm pretty sure that Paige Evans and Matt Holmes broke up. Have you heard anything about that?" I asked.

Maya nodded. "She broke up with him last week. She's got a new guy. He's a freshman at Vanderbilt."

"Wow, so it's still pretty raw. No wonder he looked so upset this morning."

Maya tilted her head and gave me a devious smirk. "Maybe he needs a little comforting. I bet you're up for it."

"Yeah right." I bit down on a hummus-laden carrot, talking with my mouth full. "The guy doesn't know I'm alive."

Maya leaned in toward me, her brown, wavy hair spilling out from behind her shoulders and brushing against the table. "Then you need to change that. Make him notice you."

"I don't know how to. Plus, he probably already has a long list of girls on his radar that doesn't include me."

"Add yourself to that list, then. Trust me, guys don't care about the whole popularity thing as much as girls do. They only care about one thing, and you know what that is."

Maya had a brother who was just starting out at Ohio University, so I figured that her musings on the inner workings of the teenage male brain were more informed than mine.

"So how did you find out about Paige and her new boyfriend anyway?" I asked.

"I overheard her talking about him during second period. She's in my Spanish class. Apparently, they met in Costa Rica last month while volunteering." Maya used her fingers to make air quotes when she said *volunteering*. It was what all the rich kids did during the summer to strengthen their college applications, usually in tropical, beachy locations. "She went on and on about how he's coming up here this weekend. I guess her parents will be in Sonoma for a wedding and they're letting her stay home. She's having a party."

"Wow, you overheard a lot. Were you guys even learning Spanish?"

"Mr. Braun was a few minutes late getting started. He and Ms. Rose were giggling out in the hallway. It was very flirtatious. I think you're going to like her by the way. I had her for American Lit last period."

"I have her next period," I said. The bell rang. We both stood and walked into the crowded hallway together. "I wonder if Matt will be at her party."

"Paige said she invited him. I guess she feels bad about breaking up with him and wants to set him up with somebody."

"Damn," I said, nudging Maya in the ribs with my elbow. "What are you, an undercover agent?"

"I can't help that Paige and her cronies were gabbing so loudly. Besides, you wanted to know."

"I guess I did. But it's stupid. It's not like any of this makes a difference in my life."

We huddled shoulder-to-shoulder as we walked the halls and up the steps, avoiding collisions in the narrow stairwell. A few yards outside of Ms. Rose's classroom stood Matt Holmes, leaning back against his locker, looking at his phone. A lock of light brown hair fell into his left eye. It really bothered me, seeing that clump of hair in his eye, and I imagined myself walking up to him and gently stroking it out of the way. I imagined that he would smile at me, and then lean down to...

"There he is," said Maya, thrusting me back into reality. "Listen, Darcy, you've got this. We just need to find a way to get invited to Paige's party."

Maya was right. For months, I'd been hopelessly pining over a boy who I never thought would have any interest in me, but here was a chance to finally make an impression on him. I couldn't let it pass me by. If I really wanted my junior year to be any better than the previous two, I knew I'd have to take some risks.

"You're right," I said. "I'll talk to you after school."

As I turned to walk into class, I noticed Paige sitting in the front row with an empty seat next her. This was my chance, and without hesitating, I took it.

TWO

P aige was looking at Instagram photos, most of which were of a tall guy with dark hair. After a moment of scrolling, she came to a photo of the two of them together. They were at a beach, Paige's blond hair blowing in the breeze. She turned her head toward me and gave me a hint of a smile. I quickly turned my head away, hoping my gawking hadn't been too obvious. Paige looked back at her phone, and I looked down at my hands, tapping my pen against my note-book. This was why I didn't try to make friends. I hadn't even started a conversation yet, and I was already embarrassed.

"Phones away now, unless you'd like to donate yours to me or one of the many other teachers here who've been using the same one since 2012 and would certainly love to have a newer model." A young woman with a wavy, red bob wearing a form-fitting, beige dress dropped a stack of books onto her otherwise clear desk. All around my classmates slid their phones into their backpacks or pockets. I guess no one wanted to call her bluff.

"Hello, scholars." Ms. Rose leaned back against her desk and faced the class. She held up a sheet of paper and took roll, writing a little note next to each name after calling it out, presumably to help her remember what everyone looked like. After she finished, she set the paper down on her desk and folded her arms across her chest. "Welcome back to school, everyone, and welcome to American Literature. Obviously, you're here to read some of the greatest American novels, stories and poems, but that's not all you're here for." She paused for a few seconds, looking around at our faces before continuing.

"You're also here to grow; as readers, as writers, as scholars, and as people." I looked over at Paige, who was gazing up at Ms. Rose attentively. On my left, Tristan Ivanov was grinning from ear to ear. I could only imagine what kinds of thoughts he was having about our young, beautiful teacher. Everyone, it seemed, was interested in Ms. Rose, in one way or another.

For the next fifty minutes, Ms. Rose talked about her love of reading and getting lost in stories. She talked about her favorite novels, which included *Beloved, To Kill A Mockingbird, and Little Women*. She talked about finding her path in life; majoring in English in college, moving abroad to teach English, first in

South Korea and then Portugal, and eventually getting a Master's in Education from Miami University and landing her job at East Point Prep. Her demeanor was poised, yet warm and casual. She didn't need to play any videos, write on the board, or even pass out a syllabus. She just talked, and we listened, attentively.

"So that's what defines me," she said as we neared the end of the period, "my love of literature and the power of the written word to transform our lives, the way we feel about ourselves and our role in society, its ability to change the way we relate to one another, to provide a perspective we wouldn't otherwise consider. And of course, my passion for teaching, and sharing the literature I love with all of you, because you guys are the future. No pressure or anything, but without you, without your compassion and desire to make an impact, there's no hope for the human race."

I looked around the room. Were we really capable of saving the global population from self-destruction? There were some really bright people in the room, like Natalie Suarez, who was destined for Harvard or Yale with grades and test scores alone. But what could any of us do to prevent the environmental calamities, food shortages, and widespread disease and war that were sure to come in our lifetime?

My only plan was to work damned hard for as long as possible so I could save up to build an underground bunker in the middle of nowhere, stocked with canned food and first-aid supplies. And then what would be the point of my fancy East Point Prep education if I was living with my mom in a bunker just trying to survive? Maybe it was all a lesson in perseverance. Just thinking about it gave me headache.

"So enough about me," continued Ms. Rose. "Now I want all of you to think about yourselves, which shouldn't be too difficult, right?" With that we all chuckled. Most stereotypes about teenagers held some truth. "Now that you understand what defines me, think about what defines you. What drives you? What inspires you? What makes you unique? You'll need to answer these questions in the form of a four-page essay. Your first draft is due in three weeks. You can find a detailed description of the assignment and a rubric online."

The bell rang and everyone began checking their phones and packing their bags. "I know what defines you," said Mitch Becker to Tristan, throwing a crumpled-up piece of paper at him. "Dumb jock."

Tristan turned around in his chair, flinging out his fist and hitting Mitch in the shoulder. "That's better than incel loser."

Mitch rose from his chair and shoved Tristan from behind. "I'm not an incel, you asshole."

"That's enough, boys," shot Ms. Rose. "There will be none of that behavior in my classroom." They both muttered an apology and walked out of the room before continuing their scuffle in the hallway.

Paige, who seemed completely unfazed, had gone back to looking at her phone. She scrolled with one hand while absent-mindedly packing her bag with the other. I took a deep breath. It was time to jump into the deep end. "So, Paige," I said, trying not to sound too eager. "How was your summer?"

"It was good. How was yours?" she asked, looking up at me just briefly before going back to what she was doing. I had the feeling she didn't actually want to hear about my summer, but had asked to be polite.

"It was fine. But actually, there was something else I wanted to ask you about."

"Yes, Matt and I broke up, so he's single now. Fair game."

I gulped, feeling my cheeks flush. I wondered if my crush on Matt had really been so obvious, or if she had just assumed. "No need to be embarrassed. You're not the first person to ask," she said.

"Oh, yeah, well there was actually something else I wanted to ask about."

Paige rose from her chair, slinging her backpack over her shoulder. "I have to get to my next period."

"I can walk there with you. I'll make it super-fast." I quickly stood up, fumbling for my bag. "So, this request isn't really for me. It's for my friend, Maya. You know her, right?"

Paige nodded. I followed her out of Ms. Rose's classroom and down the hallway to the right, the opposite direction from where my next class was. "So, the thing is, she overheard you talking about a party that you're having this weekend, and she really wants to go. She thinks the guy she likes will be there."

"Who?"

"Uh..." I quickly tried to think of a guy other than Matt who would likely be at the party. I knew that Maya wouldn't like this, but hopefully she would understand. "Tristan, actually."

"Tristan's a player," said Paige. "Tell her not to waste any time on him."

"Well, I've tried, but you know how it is when you have a crush."

Paige stopped in front of the door a few classrooms down. She looked at me, a perplexed expression on her face. "I—"

"Look," I said, before she could object. "I know we're not exactly in the same circle, and you wouldn't normally invite me or Maya to your parties, but I have a proposition for you."

"Ok, what is it?"

"Parties can get out of control, right, and messy. Spilled beer. Vomit. Trash left all over the house."

Paige shrugged. "Yeah, I guess that could be an issue."

"I'll clean it all up afterwards, for free. All I want is an invitation, for me and Maya."

She paused for a few seconds as I stood there with sweaty palms, completely regretting my decision to approach her. I was just about to tell her it had all been a joke when she finally smiled at me. "I guess cleaning is your specialty. So yeah, you guys can come, if you get rid of all the evidence."

"Deal," I said, sticking out my hand.

She gave me a half-hearted shake. "I'll give you the details tomorrow," she said before turning to go into her class.

I gave her a wave then quickly turned the other way to get to my German class before the next bell rang. In a way, it felt like an out of body experience—talking to Paige, finding a way to get myself invited to her party. My new mindset was already paying off.

Adrenaline overtook my body as I went from a fast-paced walk to a light jog. I knew I had only been given access to East Point Prep's elite on the condition that I clean up after them, but I pushed that thought aside and tried to let the joy of a successful mission linger. Next mission: go to Paige's party and talk to Matt Holmes.

I got to my German classroom and found a seat right in the middle just as the bell rang. The teacher, Mrs. Spencer, handed out our textbooks and told us to recite the list of vocabulary words on page ten. Matt sat at a desk in the front, left corner of the room. My stomach fluttered. In just a few days I would have my chance to catch his eye, maybe make some conversation, and put myself on his radar.

I imagined a few possible scenarios. I could tell him a joke in German, which seemed clever and fun, considering we were in the same German class. But then I thought that might be too corny or desperate. In addition to being the cleaning girl, I would become the awkward German girl. Then I thought I could initiate a conversation under the guise of wanting to put in a good word for a friend with a crush on him (Maya), but I couldn't keep throwing her under the bus, and there was a chance the plan could backfire and he would actually end up falling for her over me. *Stop overthinking*. The class turned the page in the textbook.

"Guten Morgan ," I recited with the class. "Mahlzeit. Guten Abend. Gute Nacht."

But the more I thought about it, the more pathetic my excitement seemed. The butterflies in my stomach flitted away, leaving a knot in their place. Maybe going to the party was a terrible idea. Chances were, even if I went, Matt would be talking to other people the entire time, and who was I to just insert myself? At best I'd be met with uncomfortable stares, and at worst mockery and ridicule. I thought back to the assignment from Ms. Rose. *What defines you? What makes you unique?* Unfortunately, what made me unique was also what made it so hard to socialize. For two years, I'd been the only student cleaner at East Point. And in two years, I'd only made one friend. It seemed unlikely for those two facts not to be linked. No one wanted to socialize with the school cleaner.

"Mein Name ist Johanna."

It was hopeless.

"Wie heißen Sie?"

No, it isn't hopeless. You're going to the party and you're talking to Matt Holmes.

THREE

I found Maya at her locker after school ended for the day. "We're going to Paige's party this weekend," I whispered.

"What!" she snapped, turning around to face me. "What do you mean? Don't we have to be invited?"

"We are invited! Paige is in my lit class. I talked to after class, and she invited us both."

I thought about explaining my arrangement to Maya, but decided against it. First of all, I didn't want her to feel guilty or like she had some duty to help me with the clean-up, and secondly, I kind of wanted her, and everyone, to just see me as a normal and cool person who got invited to parties for being liked, not because they'd had to bribe the host.

"I can't believe it!" said Maya. "I mean, you're an awesome person and why shouldn't Paige talk to you and invite us to her party? It's just..."

"I know," I said, saving her. "I know what you mean. We're not in her clique. But maybe this year will be different. Maybe this year cliques will become obsolete."

Maya hugged me. "You're amazing, Darcy! I can't wait!"

...

"How was your first day, Sweetheart?" asked Mrs. Hammerman. She handed me the clipboard with my cleaning assignment for the day. For two decades she had worked as the school secretary, and for two years she had always made me feel warm and cozy when I stepped into the office.

"It was, well. . . significant," I said, scanning my clipboard. "From here, things could either go extremely well or horribly wrong."

Mrs. Hammerman chuckled. "Well at least it wasn't boring. You'll have to keep me updated."

I lingered for a moment, hoping to tap into the grandmotherly wisdom of Mrs. Hammerman. "This might seem like an unusual question, but if you had to define me, how would you?"

"You must have Ms. Rose for English, then?"

"You know about the assignment?"

"She's been giving out that assignment, or some variation of it, for years. It's designed to help you with writing your college admission essays."

"Oh," I said, feeling out-of-the-loop. "So, what do you think I should write about? All I do is go to school and clean."

Mrs. Hammerman put down the stack of papers she had been flipping through and looked at me. "That might be true, but all that cleaning you do, that's what allows you to go to the best high school in Cincinnati. Most of these other kids don't appreciate this opportunity, because everything they have is just given to them. But you, Darcy, you work hard for it. That gives you more character, in my opinion, and shows your determination and work ethic."

"Thanks, Mrs. Hammerman. But really, my mom's the determined one. She pulled all the strings to get me here. I'm just going along with her plan." As much as I valued her opinion, I couldn't help but think the real me was being overlooked. But it wasn't Mrs. Hammerman's fault. How else was she supposed to see me when our daily interactions were limited to small talk and discussions of my cleaning assignment?

She smiled and held up a little bowl filled with chocolates wrapped in various colors of tin foil. I took a pink one. "Just remember, you're the one taking the classes here, not your mom, and you're the one staying after every day to work."

"Thanks, Mrs. Hammerman. That was helpful." I left the office, wondering if Mrs. Hammerman was even right about me. The truth was, I didn't know if I appreciated the opportunity to be a student at East Point more than anyone else did. I often wondered if I would be happier at the neighborhood public school, where I maybe wouldn't get as good of an education, but at least I wouldn't be the loner who was excluded from every extra-curricular activity. It was something I daydreamed about often, but my time at East Point was already halfway over. It didn't make sense to switch schools anymore. I'd go from being the cleaning girl with no friends to being the new girl with no friends.

The gray and white marble flooring sparkled before me as I walked toward the supply closet. It wouldn't need polishing for at least a few more days. As I opened the closet door, I heard footsteps coming down main staircase. I looked over to see Paige, Audrey, and their friend Ava making their way toward the front exit. I held up my hand and waved sheepishly. Paige looked in my direction briefly but didn't wave back. As the trio left, I heard the unmistakable sound of snickering. *Are they laughing at me? And did Paige ignore me, or maybe just not see me?*

It was difficult to know for sure— a statement that applied to almost every pressing matter before me. Was the arrangement

I'd made with Paige going to be worth it? Was she going to constantly remind me that I wasn't really a part of her social circle, that I was only invited in because I was doing her a favor? A part of me wished that I hadn't rushed to tell Maya about the invite. Then I could still back out of the deal if I got cold feet at the last minute. But since Maya already knew she would definitely insist on us going. Now that Matt was single, there was no way she'd let up on making me talk to him. I just had to suck it up and deal with the snickering. Eventually they'd get to know me and realize I was as good as them, and then the mockery and silent treatments would stop.

I opened the closet, took out the mop bucket and cleaning spray, then headed toward the East Wing. I resisted the urge to look down as I walked the halls, but still avoided eye contact with the few lingering students who passed me. They might have been freshman, but that didn't mean they wouldn't judge me.

In the East Wing, I found an empty room with a long table against the windows where I organized my supplies. For the next three hours, I made that section of the school as spotless as I could as my favorite playlist streamed through my earbuds. I wiped down the desks and swept the floors in sixteen class-rooms, emptied all the garbage cans, swept and mopped the hallways, and cleaned the windows. I did my best to stay in the zone, avoiding eye contact with the members of the Green Club meeting in room 216, who awkwardly tried to move their back-packs out of my way as I wiped and swept around them, talking amongst each other as if nothing were interrupting their chit-chat at all.

When I finished, I went back to the main floor to return the cleaning supplies to the closet. Angela, the school's only full-time janitor, was standing in the closet, retrieving clean rags. Without Angela, my job at East Point would have been much harder, and dirtier. She handled the heavy-duty tasks, like cleaning the toilets, which I only had to cover when she was out sick or on vacation.

She stuck her head out of the closet as I approached, her blond hair pulled back in the usual messy bun and her cheeks rosy from activity. "Welcome back, kid," she said, holding out her hands. I tossed her the spray bottle and dirty rag, then pushed the mop and bucket toward her. She effortlessly caught it all and put it away for me. "Have a great night."

"Thanks, Angela. See you tomorrow," I said.

Mom was already waiting for me in the front parking lot, which was an immediate relief. When Mom worked evenings, I had to take a bus home. It wasn't the worst thing in the world, but it took way longer, and a seat was never guaranteed. And seeing Mom was as much of a comfort to me then as it had been when I was a little kid. But unlike the little girl version of me, I didn't tell her everything that happened throughout the day. There wasn't any point. If she knew what school was like for me, how ostracized I was, she'd probably feel guilty for sending me to East Point, and I didn't want that.

"How was your first day?" she asked when I got into the car.

"It was good," I said with a smile.

"How are your classes? Are they going to be hard?"

"Chemistry might be, but I'm not too worried about it."

"Me neither. A smart girl like you should have no problem mastering the periodic table."

I smiled and nodded, pulling a granola bar out of my backpack.

"Are you hungry?" she asked.

"Starving!"

"Let's get pizza."

"Tony's!"

Tony's is my favorite arcade slash pizza place in town. For as long as I could remember, Mom and I had eaten there at least once a month, usually as a pick-me-up after a long day. When we got there, we found our usual corner booth and ordered a large sausage and onion, stuffed crust pizza. Then we rummaged through our bags for quarters to play skee-ball, the only way to pass the time while waiting for food at Tony's. As we rolled our balls toward the chutes, I tried to focus on the game and my wrist-flick technique, but I couldn't stop going over the events of the day, Paige's reluctance to invite me to her party, the way she walked right by me after school without so much as a smile. I threw the ball a little too hard, missing all the holes. Only when the pizza came and I listened to my mom talk about her day at work did I stop analyzing everything.

When we got home, my mom poured herself a glass of wine and turned on a true crime show. I went to my bedroom and changed into sweatpants. I stood in front of the mirror on the door and pulled the scrunchie from my hair. My long, brown hair was creased where it had been tied up. All my life, my mom and grandparents had complimented me on how smart and hardworking I was. I got the occasional comment about how nice I looked whenever we dressed up for a special event, but the compliments were always tied to my pretty dress or nice hairdo. I was never really told that *I* was pretty, and as I stood there looking at my reflection, it was hard to tell if I was.

I pulled my phone from my backpack to text Maya. *Am I pretty? I only want an honest answer.*

She replied almost immediately. *Are you kidding? You're frickin hot!!*

I smiled, knowing she would say something like that. *But is my face pretty? I kinda think it is, but I need an objective opinion.*

Yes!! Your face is gorgeous!

I let out a sigh and sat down on my bed. Maya was my best friend. She wasn't going to tell me I wasn't pretty, but I decided to believe her regardless. *Thanks, Maya. I just needed to hear someone say that before I try to go after the hottest guy at school.*

Darcy, he is lucky that you like him. Seriously. Any guy you decide to give a chance is lucky. By the way, what are you wearing to the party?

I don't know. Haven't thought about it. You? I stood up to look in my closet, a sense of panic setting in. It wasn't often that I had to think about my outfit, given I wore a uniform to school every day and lounge clothes while at home.

Less than a minute later she wrote back. *I don't know either. I HAVE NO CLOTHES. Let's go to the mall on Saturday before the party!*

Ok. You have to give me a ride, tho. Doing homework now. See you tomorrow.

I put my phone down and ordered myself to stop thinking about anything that wasn't class related. There would be plenty of time to worry about clothes later. I took my chemistry and German books from my backpack, but I wasn't in the mood to look at either one. Then I pulled out my notebook with the quote from George Elliot on the front cover. *It's never too late to become the person you might have been.* My mom had picked it up for me at the local bookstore, and I'd been trying to save it for something important. I re-read the quote, probably for the ninth or tenth time. Somehow, it made me feel better about my

29

current situation, allowing me to envision brighter years ahead. Maybe high school just wasn't my time to shine. Maybe my time was still to come, and I'd have a successful career doing something meaningful, and maybe even a husband and a family, and I could look back at my time at East Point Prep and laugh about how much time I spent worrying about social status and completely inconsequential house parties.

I opened the notebook . At the top of the first page I wrote *Things that Define Me.* Underneath I made a list.

Determined Student (Thanks, Mrs. H!)
Hard-worker
Loyal Friend
Considerate Daughter
Best Cleaner at East Point Prep (sad face)
Tony's Pizza Lover
Feminist (Duh)
Wanna be Climate Activist
Social Media Influencer (LOL)

I knew I still had some time to iron things out, but I didn't think that any of the items on my list (the ones that actually applied to me) were going to lead in the direction I wanted my essay to go. If only I were an elite athlete—I could define myself as captain and leader of the state champ girls' soccer team. Or a math genius or the daughter of a CEO who could travel the world serving humanity.

But I wasn't those things. I was Darcy Walsh, average high school student, cleaner at East Point Prep. Maybe better days were on the horizon, days when I'd be able to confidently define myself and claim my identity, but waiting for them felt like waiting for a downpour during a drought. I needed it to rain, and soon.

FOUR

O n Saturday morning I woke up with a knot in my stomach. All week I had vacillated between excitement and dread when thinking about the upcoming party, and now that it was the morning of, dread had fully taken over.

Mom was in the kitchen wearing her scrubs, pouring coffee into her travel mug in preparation for her weekend shift. "Good morning, Darcy. You want some breakfast?" she asked.

I shook my head. "No, thank you. I'm not hungry yet." It wasn't like me to skip breakfast, or any meal, but I didn't feel like my stomach could handle food right away.

"Ok, well we have plenty of cereal and eggs in the fridge if you want to fix something later. Any big plans today?" she asked me.

"Maya wants to go to the mall. And we're both going to a friend's house later."

"Oh. Which friend is that?" The elevated pitch in Mom's voice revealed how excited she was to hear about a possible new friend.

"Her name is Paige, but it's not a big deal. It might be just a one-time thing."

"Big deal or small deal, I hope you'll have fun. What time are you going?"

"Around eight."

"I should be home by seven today, so just let me know if you need a ride."

"Maya's driving, but thank you."

My mom kissed the top of my head my head. "Ok, then. I'm off to work. I'll see you later. Make sure you eat something soon. No junk food unless you eat something healthy first."

"I know. I know. Have a good day at work."

I walked into the living room and plopped down on the couch. I found the TV remote under a cushion and scrolled through the Netflix offerings. *The Perfect Date*, *Everything, Everything*, *The Edge of Seventeen*, *Alex Strangelove*. I'd already seen them all, which probably meant I was watching too much TV. I turned it off and entertained the idea of idea of getting out my school-work when Maya texted me. *I'm up. Ready to go to the mall?*

Give me 20 min to get dressed, I replied.

OK. See you in 20.

I went to my room and changed into a pair of black leggings and my mom's old MTV T-shirt that she'd given me, along with a slew of 90s band shirts. She insisted that she'd gotten too old for them, and I took them happily. The Nirvana one I had given to Maya, since she actually listened to them more than I did. It felt good to own something vintage that was actually considered cool by my peers.

After I was dressed, I combed my hair back into a ponytail and went out to the front porch to wait for Maya. She arrived a minute or two later, the windows of her 2010 Honda Civic down, a punk song with unintelligible lyrics blaring from the speakers. Riding with Maya, who'd had her driver's license for three months, was always an adventure.

"When are you getting your license?" she asked as she drove down my street toward the main road, taking the speed hump a little harder than she should have.

"What? Don't you enjoy the privilege of being my chauffeur?"

"Of course! But at some point, you might actually want to go somewhere without me."

"Nah," I said. "Plus, my mom mentioned something about trying to get me a car as a graduation gift, so I'll probably wait until then."

Maya shrugged. "I guess that makes sense."

She flew over another speed hump. "Sorry! I totally didn't see that one."

"Maybe I should go ahead and get my license now. I'll just drive you around in your car so you don't wreck it."

She jabbed me in the arm with her elbow. "Maybe that's a good idea, though."

When we got to the mall, Maya pulled into a spot right in front of Nordstrom. "You ready?" she asked, as we got out of the car. "My parents actually gave me money. I might be able to buy an entire outfit."

"I'll help you shop, but I'm not getting anything. Unless you want to buy me a present."

"The outfit you have on now looks cute. You should wear that tonight."

"Maybe," I said. "Or I might raid my mom's closet. She has some decent tops."

Once inside Nordstrom, I followed Maya to the junior's department—a maze of mannequins, sparkly accessories, and racks of black, white, and pale pink clothing. I found a large pillar to lean on while Maya rummaged through the sweaters.

"You do know it's still eighty-five degrees out, right?" I asked.

"Yeah, but they're cute. And I don't look good in anything sleeveless. My arms are too fat."

"Yeah right." I rolled my eyes at her self-deprecating remark, even though she wasn't looking. In reality, her arms were toned, stronger than mine for sure. I would wear nothing but tank tops if I had them.

"Did I tell you Harry has a girlfriend?"

"No," I said, a pang of jealousy hitting me. I'd always thought Harry was cute, but knew I didn't have a chance of dating my best friend's older brother, so I tried my best to conceal my crush (I was far more interested in Matt Holmes, anyway).

"Yeah, she was at our house for dinner last night. She's also from Cincy, so they both came back this weekend. She's nice, but I have to say, I think he can do better in the looks department."

"You do know there's more to people than looks, right? Maybe he admires her personality and intellect."

"Maybe, but she hardly talked so it's hard to say."

"I bet she was just nervous. It must be intimidating, meeting your boyfriend's family for the first time. Not that I'll ever experience it."

"You will. Trust me. Who knows? Maybe it'll be Matt's family you be meet soon."

"Shhh!" I threw a crumbled-up receipt from my purse at her. "What if someone from our school is here?"

Maya and I both looked around. "I think it's safe. We're the only ones here."

"And what about you meeting Nick Gentile's family?" I whispered.

Maya waved her hand dismissively. "It'll be a miracle if we ever get to that phase. And I mean a miracle for him."

Nick was the guy that she'd had a brief but intense fling with over the summer. They'd met while volunteering at a kid's drama camp at East Point, and for about a week he'd showered her with affection and adoration, but once the camp ended, he'd ghosted her. Now he was begging for another chance, insisting that he'd just gotten nervous about the responsibility of being a boyfriend but wouldn't let her down again. We were both a little skeptical, though. Maya pulled a tiny silver dress from a rack and held it up to her body. "Too sexy?" she asked.

"Is there such a thing?"

"You know I could never really wear this," she said, putting it back on the rack.

After what seemed like hours, she settled on a pair of heavily ripped black jeans and a cream-colored corset top. "Now I just need shoes," she said.

"I need nourishment first," I said. Skipping breakfast had finally caught up to me, and now that I was with Maya, I felt less nervous.

We made our way toward the food court. I had exactly ten dollars in my purse, which was enough to buy a burrito bowl from Chipotle, but I also loved the peanut butter smoothies from Fresh Stop. I knew I could only choose one, and Chipotle seemed like a better choice, considering all of the major food groups would be represented in one meal.

I met Maya at a table after buying my bowl, where she was already halfway through an Auntie Ann's pretzel. I checked the time. It was 12:10. In eight hours we would be at the party. It was time to hype myself and manifest good things. I could either sabotage my chances of having fun by feeling nervous and out of place, or I could assume that I belonged as much as anyone else and try to enjoy myself. Or just not go at all, but then I'd go back to school on Monday and see Matt with a new love interest and get mad at myself for not giving myself the chance to be her.

"So, here's the plan," I said to Maya. "Paige's parents told her that she could have a couple of friends over while they were gone so she wouldn't be alone in the house, but she's not allowed to have a party. That means the way we come and go will be important, so we don't get her in trouble." I took a large bite of my burrito bowl and chewed quickly to continue with the instructions. "They have one of those fancy doorbells with a camera, so we cannot go in or out through the front door.

There's also a security camera above the backdoor that faces the backyard, so we can't go that way either."

"Geez," said Maya. "What is this, Ocean's Eleven?"

"You know how rich people are with their security. Anyway, there's a side door on the East side of the house, or the right side if you're facing the front, that has no camera. We can only go in and out through that one door, and we can only approach the house from that side."

"Ok, that seems easy enough. Do they have cameras inside?"

"Paige knows that there's one in her dad's office, which will be locked anyway, and one in the front entryway, but we should be fine in the kitchen and the back part of the house."

"This is exciting. I hope no one gets too drunk and forgets all the rules."

I shrugged. "It won't be me, or you. I'll make sure of that."

After we finished eating, Maya bought a pair of black suede ankle boots to complete her outfit, then we headed back to her car to go home.

"What are you going to write about for the defining yourself essay?" I asked as Maya took the circuitous path toward the exit of the parking lot.

"What?" she asked, sounding distracted.

"You know, the essay for Ms. Rose."

"Oh yeah. Um, I'll probably go with theater, since I did the drama camp and was in Midsummer last year, and I'm getting involved with the Drama Club this year, so that should give me enough to write about. What about you?"

"I don't know," I said, leaning my head against the window. "I don't do anything interesting."

"What do you mean?" said Maya, slowly rolling through a stop sign. "You clean the school every day so that you can get an education at a private school that you wouldn't otherwise be able to attend. Colleges love that stuff."

"I guess." I knew she had a point, as did Mrs. Hammerman, but cleaning wasn't important to me, and I couldn't imagine writing an entire essay about it. But if cleaning wasn't a compelling enough topic, what else was there? The answer remained elusive. Maybe it was time to stop waiting for the rain and accept the reality of the drought.

FIVE

L ater that evening, after eating Indian food in front of the TV with my mom, I went to her bedroom closet and began assessing her collection of vintage blouses.

"Mom, can I wear one of your tops?" I yelled to her. She was still on the couch, drinking wine and watching *Unsolved Mysteries*.

"Be my guest," she answered.

I picked a multi-colored hippy style top with long sleeves that tied in the front with a bow. I'd only ever seen Mom wear it once, on one of her rare nights out with some co-workers. I got dressed pairing the top with a pair of high-waisted jeans, revealing just a slight amount of midriff. Then I applied some eye makeup and put on a pair of strappy sandals. When I was ready, I headed back out to the living room.

"Wow. You look great," said my mom. "You should just keep that top. It suits you much better than me."

"Thanks," I said, sitting on the couch. A pang of guilt hit my stomach as I thought about her sitting on the couch by herself all night. "I'm sorry for ditching the house tonight. You won't be lonely, will you?"

She smiled and paused her show. "I won't be lonely. I like having you in the house at night because I know where you are and I know you're safe, but I also want you to have fun. You work hard. I think it's good that you're letting loose a little." She put her hand on my knee, and I leaned in to give her a hug. It wasn't the first time I'd left the house on a Saturday night, but it was the first time I'd gone out on a Saturday night without needing my mom to give me a ride to my destination, which was usually just Maya's house. I told myself she was right, and that I was probably just looking for another excuse not to go. Of course she would be ok by herself for one evening. I needed to stop working myself up.

Maya pulled her car into the driveway. "Go have fun," she said. "If I don't hear from you by midnight, I'm calling a search party."

"Ok," I said as I stood up to leave. It was the first time she had needed to give me a curfew. Midnight was four aways. For four hours I needed to be a confident extrovert. I could do it.

...

Indian Hill was the most affluent suburb of the city, one that neither Maya or I ever had a reason to visit. Of course, Paige lived here.

"These houses are crazy big," said Maya as she turned onto Paige's street.

"I know," I said, ogling the mansions and their immaculate lawns. Just ahead was a row of parked cars. "I think we're getting close to her house. Park behind these cars here."

We got out of her car and walked toward Paige's house. I stopped when I saw Matt's car parked a few spots ahead, feeling my stomach churn. "Maya," I grabbed her hand to stop her. "Maybe we should just go see a movie instead."

"Why?" she asked. Then she saw the look on my face, and the car I was staring at.

"Oh, are you nervous?"

"A little," I said. I took a deep breath, and decided to tell her the truth about how I got us invited, including the part about her supposed crush on Tristan Ivanov, at which she rolled her eyes. "What if everyone makes fun of me?" I asked. "What if Paige told everyone about how I'm only coming so I can clean for her? What if I try to talk to Matt, which was basically the whole purpose of doing this, and he flat out rejects me in front of all the most popular kids? I'll never be able to go back to school if that happens."

"That won't happen," said Maya, squeezing my hand. "And if it does, I won't go back to school either. We'll just do homeschool together, which will be way more chill anyway."

I laughed, knowing she meant what she said. Maya always knew how to ease my anxieties. "Ok," I said. "Let's go."

We cut through the grass of Paige's front lawn to go to the side door. It was just starting to get dark, and as we neared the rose bushes on the side of the house, motion lights turned on, which made Maya jump. "It's ok," I said. We took a few more steps, Maya nervously looking around. "Should we knock or just go in," I said once we were standing at the door.

"I don't know," said Maya. "Do you hear anything?"

I held my ear up to the door. Silence. "No," I said.

"Maybe everyone's on the other side of the house. Paige probably won't hear if we knock. Let's just see if it's open."

I slowly turned the knob, slightly worried that this whole thing was a prank and that I would set off an alarm and get us both arrested for breaking and entering. But the door opened, and no alarm went off, so I continued pushing it and slowly stepped inside with Maya just behind me. We stood in what looked like a smaller version of the castle library in the Disney rendition of *Beauty and the Beast*. There was a cozy reading nook to the right, a fireplace to the left, and rows of books all around, complete with a sliding ladder. Straight ahead was an open door, and as we walked toward it, the sounds of music and laughing became louder.

"Here we go," I said. I took in a deep breath in walked through the door.

We stepped out into a hallway and took a right turn, following the sounds. I grabbed Maya's hand and pulled her along behind me. When we reached the end of the hallway, we entered the kitchen, which was already cluttered with red Solo cups and various kinds of beer cans and bottles.

Leaning against the counter top was Tristan, who was cracking open a Miller Lite. "Whoa," he said. "The hot cleaning girl and the cute rocker chick. Right on."

Maya and I looked at each other. She rolled her eyes so hard they practically fell back into her face, but I couldn't help but at smile at the fact that a guy had just called me hot. "Where's Paige?" I asked.

"Back there," he said, gesturing toward the adjoining room with his head. "You ladies want a beer?"

"No thanks," snapped Maya. We walked around the large island and toward the doorway that led to the other room.

"Darcy! Maya! Come on in," said Paige. She was sitting on a luxurious looking leather sectional, snuggled up to her new boyfriend, whose name I'd learned was Tom. Next to them were Audrey and Ava, who both looked up and smiled faintly but didn't say hello. They were looking at something on Ava's phone, smirking, presumably at whatever was being displayed on the phone and not at me and Maya, but of course I couldn't be sure. A sultry song played through the surround-sound speakers. It sounded vaguely familiar, but I couldn't remember where I'd heard it.

"Hey," I said, pleasantly surprised with how warmly Paige had greeted us.

"Tom brought wine coolers for the ladies," said Paige. "They're

really good. Do you guys want one?"

"Sure! That sounds awesome!" said Maya.

Paige stood up and walked into the kitchen, then came back with three bottles of a pinkish, red substance with palm trees on the labels. She handed one to me and Maya. "Cheers," she said as we all clinked the tops together.

I took a small sip and was surprised by how sweet it was, the alcohol nearly impossible to detect. Maya was practically gulping hers down, like a marathon-runner rehydrating after a race. "Slow down," I said under my breath, nudging her with my elbow.

"It's fine," she said. "I've had these before, with Harry."

"So, a lot of people are in the basement," said Paige. "It's really nice down there. My dad has it set up as his man-cave. I'll show you down."

It appeared we had no choice, so we followed Paige back into the kitchen and down a set of carpeted steps. At the bottom of the steps was a large, open room with a pool table in the middle, couches on either end, and an ornate, wooden bar along one side. "Behave yourselves," called Paige as she went back up the stairs, like a mom dropping her children off at daycare.

I looked around, trying to decide where to go. Both couches were occupied and the bar and pool table had crowds gathered around them. A football game was playing on the TV behind the bar, eliciting loud chants and howls from several of the guys.

"I hate football," said Maya, whose bottle was now empty. "I need another drink."

"I got you," said a voice from behind us. We both turned around, and as if in a dream, there stood Matt Holmes, holding two wine coolers. They were different from the ones Paige had given them. Perhaps he'd brought them himself. "I'll trade you," he said, handing a fresh one to Maya and taking her empty. "How 'bout you," he said, looking at me. At me. Talking to me.

After taking a minute to process what was happening, I quickly finished my drink, not wanting to miss an opportunity to take one from Matt Holmes. "Thank you," I said, handing him my empty bottle, feeling his fingertips graze the bottom of my hand. Both Maya and I stared at him, ready to take in his next words or watch his next move, as if he had the answers to all of life's mysteries.

He set the empty bottles down on a small bookcase against the wall and pulled a Miller Lite from his back pocket. "I don't really like football either," he said.

We all laughed. "Sure," said Maya.

"I'm serious," said Matt. "I haven't really liked football since I was in middle school."

"Then why do you still play it?" asked Maya.

"I don't know. I guess because I'm good at it, and my friends want me to stay on the team. Plus, it will probably get me a good scholarship."

Say something, I thought to myself. But what? I couldn't think of anything.

"So, what do you like then?" asked Maya.

Matt tilted his head. "That's the same question I've been asking myself for the last week. Hopefully I figure it out in time to write something for English class."

"Oh yeah," said Maya. "Darcy and I were just talking about that assignment earlier today." Maya was gesturing to me like a girl from the Price is Right showcasing a new car. It was obvious that she was trying to get me to say something.

"That's true," I said. I forced myself to make eye contact with Matt. "I'm not sure what to write about either. I mean, there are so many things I feel passionately about."

"You're the one who cleans after school, right? To get discounted tuition?" he asked.

"Yeah," I said, trying to hide my panic. This was *not* how I wanted my first conversation with Matt Holmes to go.

"You should write about that. I mean, you're the only one at the school who does it, and it shows how hardworking you are. I guarantee colleges are going to be all over that."

"That's what I said," said Maya, a little too excitedly for my pleasure.

"What about you?" said Matt, turning his attention to Maya.

I took a swig of my drink, and felt my head spin a little. It was probably time to slow down, and time to escape the conversation, which clearly wasn't going in my favor. I needed a time-out, a chance to get a handle on my emotions and re-strategize. I set down my bottle and murmured something about finding the bathroom, but couldn't tell if either Maya or Matt noticed me walking away.

I cringed inwardly over the conversation with Matt as I walked up the stairs. It had only taken about thirty seconds for my cleaning scholarship to come up, and then it seemed there was absolutely nothing else to say. When I got to the top of the steps, Tristan was still in the same spot where he'd been before, sipping a beer. My face must have shown a look of worry or confusion.

"Are you ok?" he asked.

"Yeah, I'm just looking for the bathroom."

He leaned forward and pointed down the hall we had entered earlier. "It's that way, across from the library," he said.

"Thanks," I said. I went into the bathroom, spending a few extra minutes looking at my reflection in the mirror as I washed my hands. Should I have worn more makeup? Less? More jewelry maybe? Before leaving my house, I thought I looked great, but now I wasn't so sure. When I walked back into the kitchen, Tristan was opening a fresh can of beer.

"So, why are you standing in here by yourself?" I asked, hoping to distract myself from my recent social failure.

He chuckled. "Because this way I don't have to get up every time I want another beer."

I nodded. "Makes sense."

"Actually, I had been considering going down to the basement, but then I saw you come up, so I figured the party was up here now."

"Ha, ok," I said, taking a few steps closer and leaning back against the counter next to him. I appreciated the compliment, even if it had been made sarcastically.

"So, are you having fun?" he asked.

"I don't know. I'm starting to think I should have stayed home with my mom."

"Are you kidding me?" he asked. "You must need a shot."

He turned around to grab a large bottle of clear liquid and two shot glasses, then filled up each one. "Here." He pushed one of the shot glasses toward me.

"What is it?" I asked.

"Whipped cream flavored vodka. You'll love it."

We clinked glasses. And without thinking, I poured the vodka into my mouth, swallowing it all in one gulp. It burned my entire mouth and throat as it went down. "I thought that was supposed to taste like whipped cream," I said.

"Well, it's still vodka," he said with a shrug. "You're kind of funny. Why haven't we ever talked before?"

"Um, because you've never talked to me before."

"Or maybe it's *you* who's never talked to *me*."

I laughed at the thought of me being the snobby one, but perhaps he did have a point. "Well, I'm a little shy and I have a fear of rejection, so..."

"Fear not, me lady," he said. "You're safe with me." A wide, mischievous grin spread across his face, making me laugh. I had to admit, as much disdain as I'd always had for Tristan and his obnoxious behavior, he was attractive. He was tall, like Matt, with reddish brown hair that was always unkempt, and dimples on his cheeks when he smiled. "Let's play a game," he said, pouring us each another shot. "Two truths and one lie. If you guess my lie, I take the shot, but if you get it wrong, you have to take it."

"Ok," I said, hoping I wouldn't actually have to take another shot. In the back of my mind, I wondered what was happening in the basement with Maya and Matt, but I was enjoying the attention from Tristan, so I tried not to think about it.

"Number one," said Tristan, "I'm a virgin. Number two, I rescued a drowning puppy over the summer. And number three, I write poetry in my spare time."

"Poetry," I said. "That's the lie."

"Take the shot," he said.

"What?" I balked. As hard as it was to imagine Tristan writing poetry, I hardly knew him, so I had to take him at his word. But I still didn't want to take the shot. "Hey, who's that coming up the steps?"

Tristan turned his head to look toward the basement door, and as he looked away, I turned my shot glass over into the sink, then quickly moved it up to my mouth.

"No one's coming," he said, facing my again. "Hey, did you just dump that out into the sink? You know, I would have taken it for you."

"I'm sorry. I just didn't want either of us to overdo it. You'll have to let me read some of your poetry, by the way, or I might not even believe you."

"Maybe someday. I keep my work pretty private."

"So, which was the lie? The puppy?" Given Tristan's reputation, it was really difficult to imagine that he was a virgin, but I kept that to myself.

He shrugged. "You lost your chance to know. Now it's your turn."

"Ok," I said. I took a minute to contemplate the most interesting and surprising facts about my life. "I don't know my dad, my grandparents are rich but disowned my mom when she got pregnant with me, and I hate Cincinnati chili."

"Wow, those are good," said Tristan. "I'm going with the first one, about your dad."

"This time you get to take the shot, or just dump it if you don't want to," I said.

"Really?" he asked. I nodded, and he threw back his shot, grimacing afterward.

"I think we're both done with this," I said, sliding the vodka bottle back into a corner under the cabinets.

"You don't know your dad?" he asked.

I shook my head, but didn't want to divulge any more details surrounding that story. I took a step forward, feeling my head spin a little.

"Whoa. I think you need to sit down," said Tristan. He took my hand and led me into the library. "It's nice and quiet in here. Do you want to sit down?" He motioned to the couch.

A part of me wondered if he was planning to make a move. I had been flattered by Tristan's attention, but I didn't think it was a good idea to go into a dark, secluded room with him. I thought about Maya and Matt again. Were they still talking? Did they even notice how long I'd been upstairs? Wasn't Maya worried?

"I should find Maya. I don't want to leave her alone for too long."

"Oh ok," said Tristan. He stepped aside to clear the doorway. "After you."

I walked back through the kitchen and down the basement steps with Tristan following behind me. When I got to the bottom of the stairs, I didn't see Maya or Matt where we'd been talking earlier, or anywhere else in the open room. That's when I noticed a door that was ajar on the far-right side. Without thinking twice, I walked toward the door and slowly opened it.

It was a wine cellar, dimly lit, and in the corner were Matt and Maya. She was leaning against the wall, her arms around his neck, his arms around her waist. As I stood there watching, he leaned in to kiss her. She tilted her face, readily accepting his affection.

For a moment, I just stood there, completely frozen, trying to process the scene that was playing out in front of me. It felt as if I'd turned on the TV in the middle of a show, having no idea how the characters involved came to be in their present circumstances. Only they weren't TV characters, but my best friend and the guy I liked, and I couldn't change the channel to make it go away.

Finally, I felt myself able to move, so I stepped back slowly, quietly closing the door. I turned around to see Tristan standing nearby, clinking his beer with another guy from the football team. I felt my face flush with anger, or maybe embarrassment, or perhaps a combination of both. Without hesitating I walked over to Tristan and grabbed his hand. "Let's go back upstairs," I said, and without another word he walked up the steps with me.

We went back into the library, which was still dark and quiet. I sat down on the couch against the wall, and waited for Tristan to sit next to me. I closed my eyes and tried to relax, hoping he would take the lead.

"I'm glad you came tonight," he whispered.

Was I glad I had come to the party? I didn't know what to think. Instead of responding, I turned my body more to face him and put my hand on his arm, letting him kiss me.

CHAPTER

SIX

I woke up the next morning in a spare bedroom inside Paige's house. If it hadn't been for the hangover and the fact that I'd slept in all my uncomfortable clothing, it probably would have been a great night's sleep. My mouth was dry and my head pounded. As I lay there, I tried to piece together the events of the previous night.

I remembered making out with Tristan in the library until someone walked in, tiptoeing across the room to the only safe door for exiting the party. "Don't mind me," said a voice I didn't recognize. Secretly, I felt relieved by the interruption. I enjoyed kissing Tristan, but I knew I didn't want to go any further, and I knew the longer it went on, the more likely we were to enter risky territory.

"What do you want to do?" asked Tristan after the anonymous person left.

"Go to bed," I said.

"How are you getting home?"

"Maya drove me, but I don't want to go back with her."

"There's an extra bed upstairs. Do you want me to take you up? You can get a ride home from someone in the morning."

I nodded. "I need to find my phone so I can tell my mom."

Tristan turned on the light and helped me look for my phone, eventually finding it under one of the couch cushions. I texted my mom to let her know I was staying the night at Paige's house, then Tristan walked me upstairs to the guest room. He stayed with me for a bit as I got under the covers on the bed. "I think I should go," he said. "My ride is leaving soon."

I caressed his hand. "Thank you for getting me to bed."

"It was my pleasure," he said. "I'll talk to you tomorrow."

"If you see Maya, will you tell her I don't need a ride anymore."

"Sure thing."

He kissed me one last time before leaving the room, which is the last thing I remember before falling asleep.

I tossed the thick, grey comforter off and sat up to look at my phone. A bundle of text messages awaited me. Two were from my mom. *Is everything ok?* She'd said last night, followed by *Let me know if you need a ride*, which she'd sent just moments earlier. I replied, telling her that I was fine and that I'd let her know about the ride once everyone was awake. The other four messages were from Maya, but my head was pounding too hard to read those just yet.

I got up from the bed and discovered an ensuite bathroom. Everything in it, from the floor tiles to the hand towels, was the same shade of grey as the comforter on the bed. Someone, presumably Paige's mother, had clearly spent some time picking out the correct shade of every object in the two rooms to create the perfect guest quarters. I splashed some water on my face to wash away the smeared eye makeup and cupped my hands to get some water into my mouth. I gathered up my belongings, made the bed back up and stepped into the hall-way, where I saw the main staircase to the right. I remembered I wasn't supposed to use them, so turned left to find the back stairs, leading down to the kitchen. Cups, cans and bottles were still scattered around the room, which was when I remembered my deal with Paige. *Right, I still am the cleaning girl.*

After searching for a couple of minutes, I found some garbage bags and paper towels in the pantry and some cleaning sprays in the cabinet under the sink. After clearing the garbage, I sprayed and wiped down the counters. Then I swept the floor.

When the kitchen was in satisfactory condition, I moved to the other rooms, doing my best to clean with the supplies I had available, all the while having flashbacks to the night before.

My face burned with anger at the memory of Maya and Matt kissing, but when I remembered how Tristan had been there to comfort me, I calmed down a little. Who would have thought I would connect so easily with a guy like Tristan? But on the other hand, who would have thought that my best friend could so easily kiss the guy she knew I liked?

"How's it going?" said Paige when she came down from her room. She was wearing a large, white tee shirt, her denim shorts barely visible from under it.

"Not bad," I said. "The mess is mostly cleaned up. No vomit or anything gross. But there are some crumbs on the basement carpet I should clean up. Where's your vacuum?"

Paige walked toward the front of the house and came back a minute later pushing a sleek Shark my way.

"Thanks," I said.

"How are you getting home?"

"My mom can come get me."

"It's ok. I'll drive you. I need to pick up some breakfast anyway."

"Great," I said. "Just give me a minute to vacuum."

I went back down to the basement and cleaned the carpet. Then noticed some spills on the bar that I wiped up before putting away all the supplies.

Paige was waiting in the kitchen with her car keys in hand and a small purse hanging across her torso. We walked out the front door, which she explained was ok since I was a girl, and it was mostly boys that her parents would be weary of. Tom, for example, who was still sleeping in Paige's room, would have to avoid the cameras at all costs.

I got into the front seat of her Cadillac, which was kept impeccably clean inside compared to Maya's car. Not a single straw wrapper or crumbled receipt could be found, as if she'd just received the car that day. "This is really nice," I said.

"Thanks," she said. "It was a gift from my parents, so I try to take good care of it." Paige took out her phone and opened up her navigation app. "Can you put in your address?"

"Of course." I typed it in, hoping she wouldn't mind how far away it was. "Here you go. It's a little bit of a drive."

"I don't mind. It's the least I can do after you cleaned up for me. It was such a relief to not worry about the mess this morning,"

I shrugged. "I guess cleaning is my specialty."

Paige laughed. "You should start a cleaning business. I bet you'd make a ton of money from people around here."

"Maybe, but I'm hoping to move on to something else after high school. Something more gratifying."

"I get that. It probably sucks to stay after school to clean every day."

"Yeah, a little, but I guess it could be worse. It takes a lot of pressure off my mom. She wants me to go to a good school, and she couldn't afford East Point Prep on her own."

"What about your dad?"

Her question took me by surprise. Lately I'd been so busy with schoolwork, cleaning, and advancing my social status, that I hadn't given much thought to my father. But oddly enough, I'd just brought him up the night before while playing the drinking game with Tristan. "I don't really know him. He was already married with a family when my mom got pregnant."

"Oh. So, you've never met him?"

"He saw me a couple of times when I was baby. And he used to send money and cards sometimes, but my mom told him to stop. She thought it would be better for him to not be involved at all."

"Wow," said Paige. She was quiet for a minute, then took a deep breath. "You know, my dad got his secretary pregnant a couple of years ago, so he's kind of in the same situation as your father. He decided to just give her a bunch of money so she could leave her job and take care of the baby. And she also agreed not to tell anyone that he was the father. It was really hard on my mom, but they both wanted to work through it, so they're still together."

Paige's confession surprised me more than any of the events that had taken place in the previous twelve hours. In all my life,

I'd never met someone who could relate to my family situation, and I never would have guessed Paige would be the first one. "Paige, I had no idea. That must have been really hard on you too," I said once I was able to find the words.

"Aside from Matt, you're the only one I've ever told. I know my parents don't want it public, so I never talk about it, which really aggravates me. I mean, I have a little brother who I might never meet and my dad has a child who he'll never provide any support for, aside from some money here and there. We all just go on pretending that he doesn't exist. Messed up, huh?"

I looked over to see Paige reaching for a pair of sunglasses and putting them on. I couldn't tell if she was trying to hide the fact that she was about to cry, or if she merely wanted to block out the sun. I reluctantly put my hand on her shoulder, unsure if she would welcome my touch, but she accepted it, without so much as a flinch. "The only reason I know is because I over-heard them talking about it one night when they didn't realize I was in the next room. When I went into the kitchen and asked them to explain they did, but otherwise they never wouldn't have told me."

"They probably just wanted to protect you. I mean, it's a really complicated situation."

"Yeah, but I'm still glad I know, even though it pisses me off. I always knew my dad's secretary as just Heather. But after finding out, I got her full name and even found her address. Sometimes I think about going to her house, getting some answers, trying to meet my little brother. What do you think? Is that a crazy idea?"

I thought for a moment about her plan. I couldn't imagine someone from my dad's family showing up at our house and demanding information. It seemed liked a potentially volatile situation, but still, I understood Paige's desire to comprehend the nature of her father's affair and meet the child who resulted from it. "Maybe you could leave a flyer on her porch about your babysitting services, see if she gives you a call. You'd want to use a different name, of course. That way you could get paid to hang out with your brother and be a part of his life, at least sometimes."

"That's genius!" she shouted. I smiled involuntarily. It felt nice to be in Paige's good graces. "Only," she continued, "she might recognize me. I never met her in person, but I know my dad has a picture of me on his desk at work, and who knows how many others she's seen."

"That's a good point," I said.

"But maybe after a few years. She probably wouldn't recognize me anymore by then. Unless she stalks me online or something."

I chuckled. Of course Paige would assume people stalk her online.

"So, do you know anything about your dad? Like, does he have money?" asked Paige.

"I'm not sure. I know he was in law school at the time I was born, so he might. But honestly, I haven't spent that much time thinking about it. I accepted a long time ago that he wasn't going to be a part of my life."

"You should find out," said Paige. "Because if he does, he owes you. Who knows? Maybe he could cover your tuition and you'd be able to stop cleaning."

"I don't think so. I mean, my mom and I, we're a unit, and bringing someone else into the picture might just mess things up."

Paige turned from Kenwood Road onto the onramp for the highway, as prompted by the voice on her navigation app. "Who knew you and I would have so much in common?" she asked.

"Yeah," I said. "Who knew?"

For a moment there was quiet, so I took out my phone and began reading through my messages from Maya.

Where did you go?

We need to talk.

Did you hook up with Tristan? He told me you're sleeping here.

I'm assuming you're ok and just crashed in the bedroom. Call me ASAP!

I heaved a heavy sigh. Calling Maya was the last thing I wanted to do.

"So, what happened last night?" asked Paige. "Is there something going on between you and Tristan?"

"I don't know," I said. "Somehow we ended up alone together, did some shots, and one thing led to another."

"Did you...?"

"No! We just kissed."

She tilted her head. "I'm confused. I thought Maya liked him."

I took in a deep breath, preparing to explain myself. "I made that part up," I said. Paige had just told me her most troubling secret, so I knew I had to be honest with her. "I said it was Maya who wanted to go to your party, and technically that's true, but it was mostly to help me out. And it was because of Matt, not Tristan. I've had a pretty big crush on him for a while now, so when I found out you'd broken up, I thought I might have a chance. But then Matt started flirting with Maya, and the next thing I knew they were making out in the wine cellar, and I knew the only way to avoid the hurt was to make out with somebody too, so. . ." I shrugged.

"That's awful," said Paige, curling her lip in disgust. "I can't believe Maya did you like that. And you should have just been honest with me from the beginning. If I'd known you were into Matt, I'd have helped you talk to him."

"I know. I know. But you guys had just broken up, and we didn't really know each other so I wasn't sure how you'd react." We were nearing the Edwards Road exit, which would take us into Norwood, my much more humble, blue-collar neighborhood, where old brick houses and apartment buildings were interspersed and squeezed together on tree-lined streets. "Why did you guys break up anyway?"

She sighed, as if she'd already explained the story dozens of times to everyone she knew, which she probably had. "Matt's a great guy and I really care about him. He was my first real boyfriend, and I feel like he knows me better than my own parents, but when I met Tom in Costa Rica this summer, we just had this spark between us that I couldn't ignore. The way he was with the kids there, so compassionate and kind, it really made me fall for him. And I always really liked Matt, but I never really felt like I was in love with him. I didn't like hurting him, but I had to do what was right for me."

Listening to Paige felt like listening to a self-help mentor more than a sixteen-year-old peer. "You're so lucky," I said. "I mean, to go from a relationship with a good boyfriend to an even better one with someone you actually love. Sometimes I think I'll never know what that's like, to love someone and be loved by them in return."

"Sure, you will," said Paige. "You're super pretty, even though you don't seem to know how to highlight your best features, but still, you're attractive. And you have a really good energy. Just wait. You'll meet the right guy at some point. And who knows? Maybe you'll get Tristan to finally settle down." Paige had turned onto my street and was pulling up to the front of my house.

I chuckled at the thought of being Tristan's girlfriend, but didn't totally hate the idea. In fact, I kind of liked it. "I don't really see that happening, but thanks. And thanks for the ride."

"Do you want to sit with me at lunch tomorrow?" asked Paige as I was getting out of the car.

I hesitated before answering, wondering if she was going to follow up her question with a 'just kidding' or a 'wait no, never mind.' But she didn't. She quietly waited for reply, her expression serious but inviting at the same time. "Yeah. That would be great."

I waved goodbye and walked into the house, wondering if her invitation was another charity case, or if she actually wanted me at her table. Either way, I no longer had a best friend, and I didn't want to pass up the chance to sit at the center table. Even if just for one day. If it was awkward or uncomfortable, I wouldn't have to do it again.

When I shut the door, my mom was sitting at the kitchen island. "Finally," she said with a heavy exhale as I walked toward the kitchen.

"Were you worried?" I asked.

"A little," she said. "That was the first time you've stayed out all night, and when you said you were staying at Paige's house, I realized I had no idea where Paige's house even is, and I wouldn't be able to just go and get you. I know you make good choices, but still, it was a little scary."

I gave her a hug, laying my head on her shoulder. I hadn't made the best choices the night before, but my mom had worried enough already. I didn't need to add to it by telling her what really happened. I had already learned my lesson. Each pounding sensation in my head was a reminder not to drink wine coolers again, at least not for a long time.

"I'm ok," I said. "We just got tired. But next time I go to a party, I'll make sure to give you the address first."

"That would make me feel much better." She stood up and walked over to the stove. "Are you hungry? I made pancakes and bacon."

"I'll take both!" My mom's homemade breakfasts were always my favorite thing about Sundays. Carbs and fat were sure to ease the hurt and confusion I was feeling, at least for a little while. My mom stuck a plate in the microwave for a few seconds to warm it and set it down in front of me at the counter. "Milk or OJ?" she asked.

"Actually, do you have any coffee made?"

"Oh, I didn't know you drank coffee," she said, grabbing a mug from the cabinet.

"I don't usually, but I think today I might need it."

"So, tell me what happened last night." She poured me a half-cup of coffee and filled the mug the rest of the way up with milk, then added a few shakes of sugar.

"Nothing remarkable. We just played pool and watched TV." I didn't like that I was lying, but how could I explain what really happened? If she knew that I'd been drinking, that I was probably no longer friends with Maya, there was a good chance she'd never let me leave the house again. "We all just got tired, and Paige's house is huge, so there was plenty of room for us to sleep there."

"Sounds like a nice evening. Do you think you'll be hanging out at Paige's house again? Or, you know, you could have Paige and your other friends over here sometime, if you want. Although I guess our house isn't as luxurious as hers probably is."

"Our house doesn't have to be luxurious, Mom. It's fine. And maybe I will." I took a loud slurp of my coffee. "How was your night here?"

"It was relaxing, until I started worrying about you. That was the opposite of relaxing."

"Agitating?"

"Yes, that's a good antonym." My mom took the bacon pan from the stove and put in the sink, then opened the dishwasher and started filling it with dirty plates and bowls while I ate. "Why don't we do something fun today, like go to the art museum, or see a movie?"

"I like that idea. Just give me an hour or two to do some home-work." I added my plate to the dishwasher and retreated to my bedroom, coffee mug in hand.

I sat on my bed, on top of the same pink and white striped comforter I'd had since I was eight or nine. I looked at my phone, contemplating whether or not to respond to Maya's messages. My chest still ached over seeing her with Matt, but as shocking and upsetting as it was, I didn't know if it was worth losing my best friend over. After all, maybe Tristan was the one for me anyway, and I should thank Maya for inadver-tently bringing us together. I still felt goosebumps, thinking of the way he had put his arm around me, the way he had kissed me.

As I sat there, typing and deleting a series of responses to her, wondering whether I should express anger or forgiveness, I received a message from Tristan. *Darcy, I had fun last night, but I don't want to lead you on. I think we should just be friends. Cool?*

It felt like a punch in the stomach. I fell back onto my bed. *No, not cool,* I'd wanted to say, but I stopped myself and tossed my phone to the other end of the bed. Should I really have been surprised? Should I really have expected to go from having only one friend in the entire school to dating one of the star football players after going to one party?

I wished I had never gone to Paige's party, that I'd never gotten mixed up with any of it. Things were so much better before, when I could admire Matt from afar, dish out the gossip with my best friend, and keep myself closed off from everyone else. I would have cleaned up after a hundred parties to get that sense of security back, but I knew it was gone for good. *What defines me now?*, I wondered. East Point Prep floor-scrubber *and* delusional social-climber? I closed my eyes and tried to imagine something happy, hoping to banish the terrible thoughts taking hold of my mind, but it was no use.

Just wake me up when high school's over.

CHAPTER

SEVEN

I dreaded going to school the next week, knowing how uncomfortable it would be to see everyone face-to-face. Aside from a brief nod here or there, Tristan barely acknowledged me. Instead, he flirted with just about every other girl he came into contact with. Maya and Matt were an official couple. They sat together at lunch, held hands in the hallways, and waited for one another at each other's lockers. Maya had called me twice in the first couple of days after the party, but when I didn't return her calls, she just gave up on reaching out and never said a word to me at school. She had become a complete stranger, like someone who'd had amnesia and completely forgotten her previous life. Or maybe I was the one who'd become a stranger to her. Either way, it was hard to believe how quickly our friendship had deteriorated without a single word being spoken about it. If it hadn't been for my developing friendship with Paige, East Point Prep would've been my purgatory.

On most days I sat with Paige during lunch, at her usual table in the middle of the cafeteria, which meant also sitting with Audrey and Ava, who tolerated me but never made any efforts to include me. Whenever I was around, they'd have their own independent conversation, as if Paige and I weren't even there.

Paige wasn't bothered by it. "They've been acting more and more like snobs," she said when I brought it up with her one day. "If they think they're too good for everyone else, let them. They'll eventually find out the hard way that they're wrong."

"I don't think it's everyone, probably just me," I said.

"Darcy, that isn't true," she'd said. "You've got to stop thinking of yourself as this complete social outcast. So, you stay after school and clean to get discounted tuition? So what? You're still smart and pretty and a good friend. You've got to drop this mentality of the whole world being against you, or you'll never be happy."

I stood in shock as she walked away toward her next period. It was easy for her to say. She was Paige, one of the most beautiful and popular girls at East Point Prep. She didn't know what it was like to feel rejection or heartache like I'd experienced. But then again, maybe she was right. Maybe the reason I had no other friends was because I hadn't tried hard enough to make any. Maybe the reason I had no sense of what defined me other than cleaning was because I'd spent too much time wallowing in self-pity when I should have been more proactive in figuring out what it was I wanted to do. One thing was for certain: I had some major soul-searching ahead of me.

That night my mom picked me up from school after my mopping and vacuuming were finished. "I need Tony's," I said when I got into the car.

"You got it," she said, and off we went, no questions asked.

We went in and placed our usual order. I walked over to the skee-ball machines but couldn't bring myself to start a game. Mom stood next to me and put her hand on my shoulder. "How are things at school? "You've seemed a little aloof lately."

I knew I couldn't keep my feelings bottled up anymore, not when she was asking directly. "School sucks," I said, turning to face her. "Maya's dating the guy I liked, and the guy who I thought liked me turns out to be more interested in just about everyone *but* me. And on top of that I have to write an essay about what defines me but I don't know what that is!"

"Come here," said Mom. She pulled me into a hug and placed her hand on the back of my head. She quietly rubbed my back as fell apart in her arms.

"Why does high school have to be so hard?" Tears started streaming down my cheeks against my will. I buried my face into my mom's shoulder, drying my eyes with her shirt. The arcade machines beeped and whirred around us, reminding me how public my emotional breakdown was, and yet I stayed right where I was, letting my mom run her fingers through my hair, caressing my head.

"You'll get through it," she said. "One day this will all be behind you, and you'll have a wonderful, happy life doing something you love. And I'll be a lonely, empty-nester with a house full of cats."

I laughed. "How far away do you think I'm going to go?"

"I don't know. I hope you won't go far, but I'll be ok if you do. I just want you to be happy."

I started to feel better, despite the fact that I should have been embarrassed for crying on my mom's shoulder in the middle of the arcade. I realized I should have confided in her from the beginning. She'd been through enough heartache to know how I was feeling. Maybe that was why she never seriously dated anyone else after my dad. She probably didn't want to go through it again.

"Mom," I said, still wrapped in her hug. "Do you ever feel like your life is missing anything?"

"No," she said, tightening her grip on me. "My life is complete with you."

"What about my dad? Did you ever wish that he was a part of our family? That he could have stayed with us?"

"At first I did," she said after a pause. "But that feeling went away after a while. As much as I cared for him, I knew that being with him long-term would have meant taking him away from the other people who needed him, and I didn't want to do that. But I knew I still wanted you. I never questioned that."

"Do you think I'll ever meet them? My dad and his other kids?"

"I don't know," she said. "Do you want to?"

"I'm not sure." I had to admit, even if it was just to myself, I had always wondered what it would be like to have siblings, other people who could relate to my life experience, who I could go trick-or-treating with and open Christmas presents with. But I knew that in reality, that wasn't what my father's older children were or would have been. There would have been no family picnics or camping trips. And if there were, I would have been the outsider, the intruder, much like how I'd felt at East Point Prep. Being a part of a larger family was just a fantasy, and one I didn't want to risk shattering.

Our waiter walked by and set our pizza on the table. "But I am sure that I'm starving. Let's go eat."

...

When we got home from Tony's I went to my room and took out my planner to get started on my homework for the night. For German I had to write a paragraph about my family, in German, using a list of requisite vocab words. Dare I include the tale of scandal and paternal estrangement? It certainly would make for an entertaining read for my teacher, but I decided against it. I kept it simple, describing my mom and grandparents and some of our family get-togethers. *Ich bin ein Einzelkind.*

I put my paragraph away in my and looked back at my planner. For chemistry, I had to read chapter five of the textbook and answer the questions at the end. I also had a sheet of exercises to complete for pre-calculus. It was going to be a late night.

I started flipping through my planner, looking ahead, mentally preparing for the forthcoming academic hurdles (but really just putting-off the present responsibilities). I had tests in history and chemistry coming up the following week, and tests in German and pre-calculus the week after. And, of course, there was the assignment for Ms. Rose that I had been simultaneously obsessing over and avoiding. The first draft was due the following week. Was there anything new to add to the list of what defined me? Sympathetic friend to popular girl, Paige Evans? Illegitimate daughter of married man with children? I could certainly write an essay on either topic, but it probably wouldn't be what Ms. Rose had in mind.

I shut my planner and tossed it aside, then tackled my chemistry homework. Chances were, Mr. Frazen, would randomly call on us for the answers, so I had to put some effort into it or risk public humiliation. I explained the difference between ionic and covalent bonds, defined the law of conservation of mass, and balanced five chemical equations, a tedious but straightforward task. After that, it felt like I deserved a break, so I took out my phone and opened up Instagram. The activity had become habitual whenever I had my phone in front of me.

Maya, who I was still connected with in the digital world, had posted what seemed like the hundredth selfie of her and Matt. Apparently, they had gotten sundaes from Goodman's, the local ice cream establishment, and were sitting outside with their mouths wide open. The caption: *I scream!* The corniness of it was enough to give me second-hand embarrassment, but perhaps I would have found it more amusing if I hadn't still been hurt and, of course, jealous. It should have been me eating sundaes and taking selfies with Matt. Or should it have been? I had to admit, as angry as it might have made me, the two of them did look happy together—in Instagram for all the pre-planned photo ops, but also in real life. After a moment of deliberating over whether or not to leave a comment, I decided against it and kept scrolling.

Next was a selfie of Paige and Tom with a sappy proclamation of love. *I miss you sooo much! Can't wait to see you next weekend!* It appeared that the photo was taken during Tom's previous visit, and that Paige was attempting to remind him of their relation-ship. Was she feeling insecure about it? He had left a reply on the photo, saying he missed her too, so it appeared that all was well with them.

Thankfully the next item wasn't a showcase of romantic affec-tion, but a post from a photo- journalist I followed. I clicked on the photo of a teen girl and read the caption, which explained that she was organizing a global protest in response to the government's inaction against climate change. Anyone who wanted to participate would skip school one day per week to march in the streets until leaders addressed the crisis and created a more impactful policy.

The girl in the photo wore her brown hair in a braid, a solemn expression on her face. She appeared small, almost frail, yet here she was inspiring a massive social and political movement, preparing to meet with some of the most powerful people in the world to discuss what was possibly the most pressing matter our entire civilization would face. Here was someone who wasn't just an influencer, but who was actually influential, perhaps in a way that would still be remembered twenty, fifty, or even one hundred years from now.

I spent some time reading the comments on the post, some supportive and some downright hateful. A part of me wanted to be her, to just leave behind the mundane responsibilities of being a student and do something that actually mattered. But I knew I wouldn't be able to handle the pressure, the scrutiny and the hate from people who didn't like what I was doing. And even if I just wanted to participate in the marches? I'd have to miss one day of school every week, which would certainly mean losing my tuition discount and getting kicked out of East Point Prep. My life would be over, and then even if the school strike worked it wouldn't matter because I wouldn't be able to go to college and wouldn't have a future anyway.

Maybe it was time to accept the reality of who I was and take everyone's advice. I picked up my laptop from my nightstand

and opened up a new document. In the center of the page, I typed out my title, *Keeping it Clean*. I contemplated a few opening sentences, but just couldn't get excited enough to make it past that point. After a few tries I pressed down on the backspace button, deleting everything on the screen. Once again, I was left with a blank page.

EIGHT

The next week I was cleaning on the second floor of the West Wing, where the junior lockers and most of my classrooms are. The whole day I'd tried to stay focused on school and not interact with anyone unless I was being called on during class. I'd put on blinders while walking the hallway, not seeing Maya and Matt holding hands, not seeing Tristan flirting with someone else. I tried not to think about them as I swept and mopped the hallways. Instead I listened to every song on *Lover* over and over again until I memorized all the lyrics and could sing along to them. I finished with the hallways and went into the classrooms, one-by-one emptying the trash bins and sweeping the floors in the classrooms. When I walked into Ms. Rose's classroom, I saw her sitting at her desk, grading a large stack of papers.

I still had Taylor playing in my ears, but when she looked up from her work I could see that she was saying hello to me from the way her mouth moved. She was donned in all black that day; a cowl neck sweater, a pleated skirt, tights and ankle boots, all the exact same shade.

"Oh, sorry," I said, taking out my ear buds. "I didn't realize you were still working. I can come back later."

"Don't be sorry. Do you still have a lot to do?"

"Just a few more classrooms to check."

"I just finished reading your analysis of "Recitatif." I could tell you had a really good handle on the story. Toni Morrison isn't always easy for high schoolers, you know."

"Thanks," I said, setting down the garbage bag that I'd been holding. "I liked the story a lot." I remembered that Ms. Rose had said not to use 'a lot' or 'lots'. "I mean, I thoroughly enjoyed it."

Ms. Rose laughed. "A lot's ok in conversation," she said. "Some of the time. Would you like to sit for a minute? Take a little break?"

"Sure." I took a seat in the desk directly across from hers, scooting it a little closer.

"So how is your junior year going so far?" asked Ms. Rose. She pushed her stack of papers aside and leaned in closer.

"It's ok. My classes are fine. Yours is my favorite right now."

"I'm so glad to hear that," she said, perking up in her seat.

"It's just. . ." I wasn't sure if I should tell Ms. Rose about my cluelessness regarding my own identity, but I didn't want to waste an opportunity to ask her for help. "I'm having trouble with the essay about what defines me."

"Which part are you having trouble with? You know, it's only the first draft that's due this week anyway. I'll give you plenty of feedback so you can revise it."

"Well, that's the thing. I haven't exactly started writing it yet. The problem is, I don't know what to write about."

"Hmmm, that is a problem," said Ms. Rose, tapping her desk with her pen. "Why don't we start brainstorming? What kinds of things are you interested in? What do you like to do when you aren't busy with school?"

"There are lots of things I'm interested in," I caught myself using 'lots' again. "I mean there are several things I'm interested, specifically environmental and social issues, but between cleaning and homework, I haven't been able to make the time to pursue activities in those areas."

Ms. Rose pursed her lips thoughtfully, nodding her head. "Yes, I can see how that would be a challenge. Your situation is a little different from that of most students here, isn't it?"

"Yeah, I guess it is."

"If you don't mind me prodding, could you tell me a little bit about your home life?"

"Oh, it's good." I said, making sure to squash any concerns for my well-being. "I live with my mom, in a house in Norwood. She's an ER nurse, so she's busy with her job, but she's really great. She wanted to make sure I got the best education, so she arranged the cleaning discount for me, and now, here I am."

Ms. Rose smiled. "And I bet she's really proud of you for working so hard here."

"She is." Suddenly I was fighting back tears. "She tells me that pretty often."

"I bet it's hard, being the only one at the school who stays after to clean, though."

I nodded. "Sometimes it is. I guess I just wish I could go to the club meetings, or volunteer somewhere, be more involved in the community somehow. Everyone keeps telling me that I should write about being the student cleaner, but that isn't what I want to define me."

Ms. Rose opened her desk drawer and pulled out a brochure. "You know Darcy, I have a few teacher friends around the area. One of them works at a public elementary school in the city. A few years ago, he started an urban gardening program there. The kids who participate in it learn about sustainability, healthy-eating, and they get access to fresh fruits and vegetables that they otherwise might not have. Do you like kids?"

"I think. I mean, I haven't spent much time around them, but sure, I guess so."

"Great, because he could use another high school volunteer to assist the kids. It might be the perfect opportunity for you. You'd be helping kids, and you'd be growing and harvesting organic produce. It checks the boxes for both environmental and social causes, right?"

"Yeah, it sounds great," I said, taking the brochure that she held out to me. "But I have to stay after school to clean every day, so I'm not sure how I could do it."

"Ah, yes." Ms. Rose folded her hands together and leaned in toward me. "Do you want to know a little secret about me?"

"Sure," I said, intrigued.

"I'm rich," she said, matter-of-factly.

"You're rich?" I repeated.

"Yes, very rich."

"Ok," I said, trying to figure out how her financial status pertained to the urban gardening program or my inability to do it.

"Not from teaching, of course. I'm a trust fund baby." She shrugged, as if the information had little significance.

"Oh, I wouldn't have guessed."

"I know," she said. "Because it was never something I wanted to define me. I like having money, but just having money isn't enough. I wanted to work. I wanted to teach. I wanted to make an impact."

"That's awesome. I wish everyone with a trust fund felt that way."

"Well, there are some who do, but not enough. And that's one of the biggest problems with society, right? The people with the most give the least? So I figured, who better to teach the young, spoiled rich kids to have some compassion than someone who can actually relate to them a little bit?"

"Yeah," I said. "That makes sense, and I'm glad you do it."

"So," she said, "you're probably wondering why I'm telling you all this."

I nodded.

"I'm going to make you a deal. If you volunteer for the urban gardening program, I'll pay your tuition for the next month. You can try a new activity, help out some amazing kiddos, and you won't have to worry about staying after school to clean because your tuition will be covered. How does that sound?"

"That sounds amazing," I said. If I hadn't been sitting in a desk, I might have leapt up in joy. "That's so generous of you. But will Mrs. Masterson allow that? I mean, there's only one janitor, and she probably expects me to stick to my cleaning schedule."

"I don't see why it will be a problem, as long as the school has the money. As important as your service is, I'm sure that we can manage without it for a month. We have plenty of resources here."

I stammered briefly, trying to find the right words to express my gratitude and excitement. "This is so amazing. Thank you so much."

"You're welcome. I think it will be a good investment," she said. "I'll talk to Mrs. Masterson tomorrow to work it all out. In the meantime, you can email Mr. Brooks and let him know you'd like to participate. His contact info is on the brochure. Tell him you're in my class. Also, don't worry about the first draft. You can turn your essay in when the final draft is due next month."

I stood up from my seat, smiling so big that it actually hurt my cheeks a little. "I can't wait." I picked up my garbage bag and moved toward the door. "I should finish my rounds for the day and let you get back to your work. Thanks, again, Ms. Rose. This is just what I need."

Ms. Rose smiled brightly. "I'll see you tomorrow, Darcy."

I left the room, clutching the urban gardening brochure like a boarding pass for a European getaway. My secretly rich teacher wants to pay my tuition for a month so I can garden and spend time with kids, I kept telling myself. I felt like I'd just won the lottery, or stumbled across a map leading to long-lost treasure. I rushed through the rest of my cleaning and returned the supplies to the closet. My mom was working late that night, which meant I was taking the bus home, but I didn't mind. Nothing could put a damper on the happiness I was feeling about my new opportunity.

"You done for the day, kid?" asked Angela. She was wheeling a mop and bucket toward the cafeteria.

"Yep," I said. "And I hope you don't mind, Angela, but I think I'm going to take a break from cleaning for the next month so I can do some volunteering. Will you be ok without me?"

"Sure thing, Darcy. In fact, I could use some extra money right now. Maybe they'll give me overtime."

"I hope so."

"Enjoy yourself, kid. You can tell me all about it when you start up again."

"Thanks, Angela. I will." I watched as she pushed the mop and bucket onto the elevator and waved goodbye before running outside toward the bus stop. Finally, the drought was coming to an end.

NINE

The next day, Ms. Rose pulled me aside after class to let me know that Mrs. Masterson had approved our arrangement. I almost jumped from excitement, but stopped myself before fully committing, realizing how odd it might look, so I ended up just standing on my tip toes and rocking forward slightly. "Thank you so much, Ms. Rose. Can I give you a hug?"

"Of course," she said. She gave me quick squeeze and then put her hands on my shoulders. I could tell that she wasn't much of a hugger, and yet she seemed pleased to grant my request. "But Mrs. Masterson did say that you have to go back to cleaning after a month, if you're going to keep your discount. I wish I could buy you more time, but with fall kicking into gear, I think the gardening program will be wrapping up a month from now anyway."

"It's perfect," I said, although I wondered if she had a point about needing more time. "But can I write my essay about something I only do for a few weeks?"

Ms. Rose smiled at me the way I imagine she'd smile at a cute kitten. "Darcy, what defines you is up to you. And it isn't just about what you've done already, it's about what you plan to do with your future, what you're working toward. And who knows, maybe this opportunity will open up some new doors for you."

"True. I hope it will." I started to walk away, but then remembered one last thing I needed to address. "Ms. Rose, do I need to tell my mom that you're doing this for me?" I asked.

"Do you think it would make her uncomfortable?"

"Well, I think she'll insist on paying you back."

Ms. Rose smiled. "I definitely will not allow that. Just tell her that Mrs. Masterson agreed to give you some time off so that you can get a little volunteer experience. Don't even mention the tuition, and hopefully she won't ask."

"Thanks, Ms. Rose. That sounds like a good plan."

As I walked out of the classroom, Paige was waiting for me in the hallway. "Darcy!" She put her hand on my shoulder somewhat forcefully, as if she thought I might run away from her. "You haven't been sitting with us at lunch lately. What's going on? Are you mad at me or something?"

I laughed, a little stunned that Paige had worried I was mad, or had even noticed my absence. Maybe my role at East Point Prep was bigger than I'd realized. "No, I'm not mad. And sorry for missing lunch. I've just been going through some stuff, and needed a little time to figure things out. Thanks for being concerned, though."

"So, are you done figuring things out?"

"Not totally, but I'm getting there." I looked around to see if anyone else was in earshot of our conversation. "Don't tell anyone, but Ms. Rose is paying my tuition for a month so I can volunteer for an urban gardening program."

"Wait," said Paige, a little louder than necessary. "She's paying your tuition? Why?"

"Shhh. And yes, she has a lot of money. It's just temporary though, so I can get some experience with something after school other than mopping the floors."

"Wow! Who knew a high school English teacher could be rich? That's great! I'm excited for you."

"Thanks," I said. After being a loner the previous week, it was nice to know I still had a friend who cared about my well-being.

"I have to get to pre-calc. Will I see you at lunch tomorrow? Audrey and Ava are getting on my last nerve and it would be great to have some stimulating conversation."

"I can't promise I'll be stimulating, but yeah, I'll be there."

"Great. It's a date then."

We both turned and began walking to our next periods. Up ahead I saw Matt walking into our German class. As I watched him, I realized for the first time that seeing him didn't make me feel anything, not a single inkling of jealousy, regret, or longing. If anything, it was just nostalgia. The crush on Matt was a part of the old Darcy, and it was time to work on shaping the new one.

...

At the end of the day, I went to the restroom to change into some jeans and an old tee-shirt that I had in my backpack, and instead of going to the office for my cleaning assignment, I went straight outside and waited for the bus to take me Downtown. I'd already emailed Mr. Brooks, Ms. Rose's friend from Taft elementary, and he'd said I could start right away if I wanted. Junior Gardeners was held every Monday, Wednesday, and Friday, and luckily it was Wednesday. I would just have to stop by the front office first to fill out some forms with the secretary and I would be good to go.

I had just enough time to get there before the after-school program started, since East Point dismissed earlier than the public schools. When the bus arrived, I scanned my pass and walked straight toward the back to an empty row of seats, where I had enough space to set down my backpack and get myself organized. I took out the brochure and read through it more carefully.

In the Taft Elementary School Junior Gardener's Program, we teach students to value nature, good nutrition and their own hard work. The Junior Gardeners take part in every step of the gardening process; tilling the soil, planting the seeds, watering and weeding, and finally, harvesting and eating the food they grow. Along the way, they learn about the science of agriculture and the importance of sustainability. Our teen volunteers assist the Junior Gardeners in each step of the process, providing support, encouragement and additional instruction when needed.

I hoped that the kids wouldn't need very much 'additional instruction.' When it came to gardening, I knew some basics, but was in no way an expert. It had been years since Mom and I had grown a vegetable garden in our yard. The last time our carrots had come out okay, but our tomatoes had been over-taken by some sort of fungus and tiny insects ravaged our lettuce. Mom didn't want to bother with it after that, but I was hopeful that after this experience I would be able to try it out again on my own.

The bus got more crowded as we got closer to downtown. I put the brochure away and put my backpack on my lap to make more room for other passengers as the bus filled up. I looked out the window at Over the Rhine, a historic neighborhood that had had recently been revitalized, with new restaurants and shops opening on almost every corner. It was the best people-watching I'd had in a long time. When the bus stopped at a red light, a man on the sidewalk bumped into a woman coming out of a bookshop. He spilled his coffee and she dropped her bag, her books falling out onto the ground. He bent down to help her pick them up. The bus rolled forward before I could see how the situation played out, but I hoped it was the beginning of a happy relationship for them.

I got off the bus in front of Washington Park and walked up Elm to 14th Street, where the school was located. A nervous nausea pounded at my stomach as I walked up the steps to the front entrance. What if this was a huge mistake? What if all the kids hated me? I probably knew far too little about gardening to provide any help whatsoever and there was a chance I would actually just destroy any plant I touched. I stopped for a moment to talk some sense into myself. *This is a great opportunity, Darcy. The kids will like you. You'll have fun and learn more about sustainability. Go make Ms. Rose proud!*

After ringing the doorbell and hearing the click of the doors unlocking, I went inside and found the front office just to the right. A portly woman with glasses was sitting at the desk with a placard that read Mrs. Walker. "I'm here to volunteer with the Junior Gardeners. Mr. Brooks told me to check in at the main office first," I said.

"Ok, honey," said the woman. She gathered some forms from different stacks and attached them to a clipboard. "We just need some information from you, so fill these out and then I'll tell you where to go."

I filled out forms with my medical history and emergency contact information, and gave the clipboard back to Mrs. Walker. "Thank you, Honey," she said. "Now you just go right down the hallway, and through the double doors on the left. Have fun. Those kids are a hoot."

"Thanks, Mrs. Walker," I said, feeling more at ease. The walls of the hallway were decorated with various art projects the students had completed, collages made with tiny pieces of construction paper and faces made with pieces of yarn and glue. Inspirational messages were stenciled on the walls in fancy lettering. *Believe you can and you're halfway there. - Theodore Roosevelt. If you can't fly then run, if you can't run then walk, if you can't walk then crawl, but whatever you do you have to keep moving forward. - Dr. Martin Luther King Junior.*

I walked through the double doors and down some stairs that led to a large lunchroom. On one side was a row of long, rectangular tables, and on the other was an open space that appeared to serve as a gymnasium. A boy who looked about my age was sitting at a table near the back wall. He lifted his head and looked at me with curiosity, his dark eyes glistening. I walked closer, trying to decide if I should say hello or wait for him to say something first.

"Are you here to volunteer with the gardening club?" he asked.

"Yeah. It's my first day. Are you?"

"Yup," he said.

I stood in front of him, teetering back and forth on my feet. "You can sit," he said. "There's plenty of room here."

I laughed, realizing how awkward I must have looked. "I'm Darcy," I said after sitting down next to him.

"I'm Sean." He was wearing an olive-green hoodie and had a notebook on his lap. The sides of his head were buzzed, with slightly longer hair on top. He was slender but tall, with inviting eyes and a striking jawline.

"What are the kids like?" I asked.

"Most of them are pretty good. I'm glad I finally have some help, though."

"Have you been doing this a while?"

"Since the beginning of the school year. I wanted to volunteer with kids, and I like being outside, so this was a good fit for me."

I looked at my phone. It was 3:28, which meant that the elementary kids would be pouring into the room in about two minutes. "So, what do we do exactly?"

Sean laughed. "You do know what gardening is, right?"

"Yeah, sort of," I said with a chuckle. "My mom and I tried it a couple of years ago but we weren't very successful. We didn't do any research or anything. We just kind of threw ourselves into it and then gave up when it didn't work out."

"I guess they should have vetted you better," he said. I must have looked nervous. "I'm just kidding. You'll be fine. Most of the plants are already doing pretty well so you don't need to worry about whether or not stuff will grow. We just take the kids out to the plots, make sure they water everything, help them make observations about their plants, and let them pick the vegetables that look ready. It's pretty chill."

"That's good," I said. We sat in silence for a few seconds, until the bell rang. Less than a minute later came a stampede of footsteps coming toward the cafeteria. A tall man with a shaved head and broad shoulders was the first to enter, followed by another man in basketball shorts and what seemed like at least a hundred kids.

"Are all of these kids Junior Gardeners?" I whispered to Sean.

"Yeah, but they get split up into three age groups, and each group goes on a different day of the week, so we're only taking the youngest ones today."

"Phew," I said.

The man in the basketball shorts wheeled out a large metal cage filled with bouncy balls, which the kids instantly ran to. Within seconds, balls were being bounced in every direction and the sound of shoes squeaking on the floor reverberated across the large room.

"Junior Gardeners," called out the tall man, who I assumed was Mr. Brooks, his voice booming. "Today it's the Kindergarteners and first-graders. Come line up next to our high school friends at the lunch tables." About twenty or thirty kids came running to stand behind him. "You must be Darcy," he said in a much quieter voice when he turned to face me.

"Yes," I said, standing up.

"Nice to meet you." He held out his hand and I shook it, feeling a firmer grasp than I'd expected. "Sean here knows the ropes. He'll fill you in on everything you need to know."

Sean looked at me, giving me a playful smirk. We both stood up from the tables, leaving our backpacks where they were, and left through a door on the back wall of the lunchroom.

When we stepped outside, we were completely surrounded by concrete and blacktop, with no garden area in site. "So, where's the garden?" I asked.

"We have to walk about four blocks, so just keep an eye on the kids and make sure everyone stays together. I usually lead and Mr. Brooks walks in the back. If you want to you can hang out in the middle."

I let Sean and a few of the kids behind him get ahead of me, then started walking again when the kids in the middle of the line caught up to where I was. "Who are you?" asked a little boy with glasses and a shirt that was at least two sizes too big.

"I'm Darcy. I'm here to garden with you. What's your name?"

"Devin," he said. "Are you Sean's girlfriend?"

I laughed, surprised that a kid so small would even be familiar with the concept. "No. I actually just met Sean today. He seems nice though."

"Yeah, he is. Can I hold your hand?"

I smiled at how quickly he transitioned. "Sure." I held out my hand, letting him wrap his little fingers around my palm. "What grade are you in?"

"Kindergarten." Our line made an abrupt stop as we reached an intersection with a blinking red hand warning us not to cross. Catty-corner to us was a middle-aged man with a bottle wrapped in a brown paper bag. He was singing loudly. No one from the school seemed to pay him any mind.

"So that must make you five or six, right?" I asked once we started walking again.

"Five-and-a-half," said Devin proudly.

As we marched on, hand-in-hand, I felt a tug on the back of my tee shirt. I turned around to see a little girl with braided hair. "Hi," I said.

"Can I hold your hand too?" she asked.

"Of course," I said, holding my free hand out to her. "I love your shoes."

"Thanks," she said. "They light up." She stomped her feet to show off the pink lights that ran along the bottom.

"That's amazing!"

The three of us walked along with the ease of ducks floating on a pond. For these kids, it didn't really seem to matter what you looked like or how old you were. Everyone had the potential to be a friend. After continuing for a couple of blocks, Sean stopped at a black iron fence that enclosed the corner lot of Vine and 15th Street. Mr. Brooks came running from the back of the line with a key to open the pad lock on the gate. "Let's go, kids," he yelled as he pushed the gate open, and all the kids went running through like scampering puppies chasing after a squirrel.

The garden was one of the most beautiful and impressive things I'd ever seen. Rows of raised beds held various shades of green plants; lettuces, tomato vines, and herbs. Between each garden bed were stones with small patches of grass here and there, and in the center was a stone path that led to a wooden gazebo in the back of the garden. In one corner was a shed for the gardening tools, and next to that was a small, manual water pump that the kids used to fill their watering cans.

"It hasn't rained in a while," called out Mr. Brooks, "so let's give these plants lots of water."

"These kids pretty much seem to have it under control," I said to Sean as we watched the little ones get to work on filling up their cans and carefully carrying them over to the plants.

"It might seem like that now," he said. "But we have to make sure they don't keep watering the same plant like fifty times while completely neglecting the others."

"Oh," I said, nodding.

"All the plants are numbered, which makes it easier to tell the kids which ones to water. Here's what I think we should do: I'll take plants one through twenty-five and you take twenty-six through fifty. You don't know all the kids' names yet, so since we have an even number of boys and girls, I say I manage the boys and make sure they water all my plants, and you manage the girls with your plants. Sound cool?"

"Oh, so you want a battle of the sexes? Ok, you're on!"

I ran to the watering pump and gathered up the girls, instructing them each to water a different plant in our section.

"Is it girls against boys?" asked Ciara, the girl with the light up shoes, after noticing all the boys were going to the other side with Sean. "We aren't really competing," I said. "Sean and I just needed an easy way to split everyone up."

"Well, I think we're gonna win anyway," said Ciara.

"Me too," I whispered, giving her a high five.

For the next ten or fifteen minutes, I helped the girls water each of the twenty-five plants I'd been assigned to, which were all located on one side of the center path. I had to make sure that they held their watering cans in the right position, so that they watered the soil and not just the tops of the plants. Joy, a chubby-cheeked girl with glasses, was the most meticulous of the bunch, putting the end of her watering can at the very bottom of each plant, moving it around to water each side evenly.

With each trip to the water pump they either squealed with laughter or shouted with indignation. "He splashed me!" or "She got my shoes wet!" But a simple reminder of which plant they needed to water next was usually all it took to quell the conflict. Keeping them on task was easy because they enjoyed their work.

After the watering was completed, Sean and I gathered the cans and returned them to the shed. Mr. Brooks, who had been setting up plates and forks at a table on the gazebo, began handing out baskets to all the kids. "It's harvest time!" he yelled. The kids bounced around excitedly, taking their baskets one by one. A few of them began to scatter around the garden, eager to get picking. "Wait, wait, wait," called Mr. Brooks. "Not yet! Wait for your name to be called so you know which plant to harvest. And please, let either me, Sean or our new friend Darcy help you out. No harvesting until you have a helper. That means you have to be…" He leaned forward, cupping his ear with his hand.

"Patient!" yelled the kids.

"That's right. You all have to be patient while you wait for your helper to come to you. And when we're all done harvesting and washing our vegetables, we'll have our feast!"

While Mr. Brooks told each kid which plant to pick from, Sean handed me a pair of shears and gave a quick run-down on how to harvest each of the plants. I learned about the 'cut and come again' method for the lettuces and green leafy vegetables, and to loosen the dirt around the carrots to make them easier for the kids to pull out.

"What if I mess something up?" I asked, a little nervous about my lack of gardening knowledge.

"Just blame it on one of the kids," said Sean.

I laughed, assuming that he didn't meant it.

"Seriously, though, you'll be fine. Just let me know if you need help with something."

"Ok," I said. "I got this. Who should I help first?"

"Why don't you help Jaycee and Cameron with the tomatoes and then help Marcus and Emberly with the lettuce. I'll be over in the green beans."

I quickly got to work, helping Jaycee and Cameron find the best tomatoes, making sure we left the ones that hadn't fully matured. Then I cut some iceberg and arugula with Marcus and Emberly. When I finished with that, there were some kids next to the carrot patch jumping up and down chanting my name, so I strutted on over like a celebrity getting ready to dole out autographs. I loosened the dirt around the carrots, then let the kiddos work their magic. Seeing the looks on their faces when they pulled them out of the ground was like seeing the lights on a Christmas tree being plugged in for the first time. They were the most genuinely happy expressions I'd ever seen.

After everyone finished harvesting, we took the vegetables to the water pump to be rinsed. Then the kids sat around the table under the gazebo while Sean, Mr. Brooks, and I cut and chopped the veggies into bite-sized pieces. Mr. Brooks mixed it all together in a big bowl.

"Salad time!" he called out. Most of the kids were excited, except Cameron, who whined that he hated salad. I put some of the sliced carrots and tomatoes onto his plate and squeezed some ranch dressing out on the side, which made him happy.

Once all of the kids had salad on their plates, we offered them dressing and helped them mix it in with their forks. Mr. Brooks also gave them little paper cups of water and passed around some pretzels. "So, this is pretty much it," said Sean, once all the kids were busy eating their snack. "We'll do basically the same thing each day but with a different group of kids. The older ones are a little more self-sufficient, so it shouldn't get any more difficult. What do you think so far?"

"It's great! This is the most fun I've had in months. Does that make me sound lame?"

"No," said Sean, biting into a pretzel. "I think it's fun too."

"More salad!" shouted Marcus.

"And how do we ask for more?" said Mr. Brooks, who'd been monitoring the kids on the other end of the table.

"May I have more salad please?"

"Much better," said Mr. Brooks. "Who else is ready for round two?"

Almost everyone's hand went up. Seconds of salad and dressing were put on their plates. The pretzels and water pitcher were passed around again too. When everyone was done eating, Sean and I helped Mr. Brooks clean up the gazebo. Then the kids lined up and we began our walk back to the school. Devin and Ciara wanted to hold hands again, so of course I indulged. For the first time ever, I wondered if I might have a future as a teacher. I had always seen myself doing something corporate and high-paying, like tax law or software engineering, but over the last couple of hours I'd finally started to feel like I was a part of something bigger, and it was something I enjoyed. I knew teachers weren't paid as much as they deserved to be, but maybe the gratification that came with the job made it worth doing.

We went back into the school through the same doors we had exited from earlier. Mr. Brooks held the door open for everyone. "Kids, you have a few minutes to play before you go home for the day," he called out. Then he turned to me. "Darcy, thank you so much for coming today. It was a big help for us, and I can tell the kids really like you."

"It was my pleasure," I said. "I can't wait to come back."

"Oh, and tell Ms. Rose she should join us sometime too!"

"I will," I said, just as he went running off toward the other end of the lunchroom to confer with the other teachers.

Sean and I retrieved our backpacks from the corner table. "Is Ms. Rose one of your teachers?"

"Yeah, she's my English teacher. She's friends with Mr. Brooks, and she's the one who recommended this program to me."

"What school do you go to, anyway?"

"East Point Prep," I said, throwing my backpack onto my shoulder. I followed Sean as he stepped outside.

"So, you're rich then," he said with a grin.

"Um, no," I said. I didn't see much point in misleading him, and I'd gotten so comfortable in the last couple of hours that I didn't feel the need to hold anything back. "I get discounted tuition by staying after school to clean. Normally, I wouldn't be able to do an after-school activity like this, but Ms. Rose is paying my tuition for the next month so I can get some volunteer experience."

"Wow. That's really cool."

"Which part?" I asked.

"The whole thing," he said. "I mean, it's cool that you found a way to go to such a good school, and it's also cool that your teacher is helping you out like that."

"Yeah, I guess so. I feel kind of embarrassed about it sometimes, though. I'm the only one at my school with that arrangement, and I feel like everyone looks down on me because of it." I looked over to see a bench a few feet away and decided to sit down. Sean sat next to me.

"Well, they won't be looking down on you when you get into an Ivy League school. Colleges recognize people in unique circumstances, especially when it shows how hard they work."

"We'll see. So, where do you go to school?" I asked, eager to steer the conversation away from me.

"The Academy for the Arts."

"Really? I've heard a little about that, but I've never known anyone who went there. What's it like?"

"Academically, it's not great, but the arts programs are some of the best in the country for high school, so if that's what you want to major in for college, it's a good place to be."

"What's your program?"

"Visual art. I draw." He took a sketchbook out from his backpack and flipped through it to give me a glimpse at his talent.

"Those are amazing," I said as he showed me drawings of several historical Cincinnati landmarks, the Roebling Bridge with all of its suspenders and cables, Music Hall and the city skyline, all done with impeccable detail.

"I prefer to sketch people," he said. "I did these for an assignment."

"Well, they're really good," I said. "I've never known anyone who could draw like that."

He shrugged. "I'm all right."

"Better than that," I said, lightly bumping his shoulder with mine. I suddenly felt self-conscious. Was I being too much by touching him, even if it was just with my shoulder? I decided to dial it back, subtly scooting away, before making a fool of myself. "So, is that what you want to go to college for?"

"Yeah, I'm hoping I'll get into DAAP."

DAAP, at the University of Cincinnati, is one of the country's most competitive collegiate art programs. Applicants typically only get in if they have high test scores, excellent grades, and impeccable artistic talent. "I bet you're a shoe-in, with drawings like that," I said.

Sean continued flipping through his sketchbook. Toward the end he landed on a drawing of a girl from the shoulders up. Her heart-shaped face was framed by long, curly locks. She had full lips, a dainty nose, and freckles at the tops of her cheeks. "Wow," I said. "She's beautiful."

"Oh, yeah. Thanks," said Sean, quickly shutting the book and putting it away. "I should probably start walking to my bus stop. How are you getting home?"

"I'm taking the bus too."

"Do you want to walk with me?"

"Sure," I said, popping up from the bench.

We headed in the direction of the park. The sidewalks were becoming crowded with youngish adults going in and out restaurants and bars. "So where do you live?" I asked.

"Hyde Park."

"Hyde Park?" I asked, picturing the large Victorian and Colonial houses that I silently fantasized about living in whenever my mom took Madison Rd. "It sounds like you're the rich one."

Sean chuckled. "Well, my parents are both doctors, so I guess they've got some money. We're not East Point level rich, though."

"Still, Hyde Park is a major step up from Norwood."

"Norwood, huh?"

I nodded. "I know it doesn't have a great rep, but our street is nice. It's where I've lived since I was in kindergarten."

Sean smiled, shaking his head. "I was just saying that because it's so close to Hyde Park. Maybe when I get my car, I'll come pick you up sometime."

My heart leapt at those words, but I tried to contain my excitement and stay cool. "You're getting a car?" I asked.

"Hopefully. Sometimes my dad lets me drive his, if he's in the right mood and isn't planning to go anywhere, but my parents said they'll get me my own car for my birthday if I stay on the straight and narrow. It probably won't be a Lexus or anything though."

"Hey, a car's a car. I'd take anything with a working engine. I'd also take a ride in anything with a working engine."

"Me too," said Sean. "Anything beats the bus."

We arrived at the bus stop just as the Hyde Park bus approached from the next block. "Good timing," said Sean. "Is yours coming soon?"

"I think so, but if it doesn't, I'll just call my mom. She's probably getting off work right about now."

"Cool," said Sean as his bus pulled up to the curb. "See you on Friday?"

"Yep," I said. I watched as he pulled his earbuds from his pocket and put them in place. Then he scanned his bus card and walked toward a seat as the doors closed.

My bus arrived a minute later. I took out my change and earbuds in preparation. After sitting down and selecting my playlist I pinched myself on the back of my hand. I'd just had the best afternoon of my life since starting high school, and it was almost too hard to believe. I'd met dozens of new people, and it hadn't even been stressful. The work had been invigorating and rewarding, and talking to Sean had been a breath of fresh air. Friday couldn't come soon enough. I put my head back against the seat and closed my eyes. Thank God for Ms. Rose.

TEN

"Darcy!" Paige shouted as I approached her lunch table. "Sit down here! I'm so anxious to hear about your volunteering yesterday. How did it go?"

"Great!" I said. I sat in the spot she's been gesturing to and starting unpacking the contents of my lunch bag. Audrey and Ava weren't looking my way, so I ever-so-slightly turned my back, putting my full attention on Paige. "I had an amazing time! The kids were really sweet. I was a little worried that I didn't have enough gardening experience, but it didn't matter at all. Especially since Sean was there to walk me through it."

"Wait. Who's Sean?" asked Paige, just before putting a bite of salad into her mouth.

"He's the other high school volunteer. He's really good with the kids, and he seems pretty cool too."

"Is he cute?"

I felt myself blush. "Yeah. But I think he might have a girlfriend." I thought of the drawing of the gorgeous girl from his sketchbook. Chances were, he'd have to spend a lot of time looking at someone to draw such a detailed rendering of them.

"That doesn't really matter. I mean, I had a boyfriend when I met Tom, and that didn't stop me from falling for him. If he does have a girlfriend, he can break up with her."

"I don't expect anyone to break up with their girlfriend for me anytime soon." Especially not ones that look like Greek goddesses. "Besides, I still hardly know him. Anyway, how is Tom?"

"Good." Paige ate another larger bite of salad. The expression on her face had changed to one of worry. "I mean, I think he's good. He's been so busy with school lately that we haven't talked very much."

"Oh," I said. "Well, I suppose college is more demanding than high school."

"Yeah," she said, "That's true." She moved her hand over her eyebrows to shield her eyes.

"Paige, are you okay?" I whispered.

She shot up from the table and quickly walked out of the cafeteria. I looked over at Audrey and Ava. Audrey shrugged, and Ava turned back to look at Paige. "Boy troubles, I guess," she said.

I waited for one of them to do something, but they started talking amongst themselves about how Paige had been better off with Matt. "She never got upset like that when she was with him," remarked Audrey.

"I'm going to go talk to her," I said, getting up from the table. I left the cafeteria and went to the hallway. Paige was up ahead, going into the girls' bathroom. I ran inside and found her feet in the last stall, which she'd already shut behind her. "Paige, are you ok? Are you sick?"

"No," she said through intermittent sobs.

"Do you want to talk? Is it something with Tom?"

She unlocked the stall and came out, her mascara smudged around her eyes. "I think he's going to break up with me," she said.

"Why do you say that?"

She walked over to the wall and sat down on the windowsill. I sat down next to her. "He used to text and call me all the time. If I messaged him, he'd reply almost instantly. But now, it seems like we only talk if I call him, and he's always in a hurry to get off the phone. He'll tell me that he'll call me later, but then he'll just send a text late at night saying he's too busy studying or something. I don't know if he's really busy or if his feelings about me have. . . changed."

"Maybe you should just ask him," I said.

"I want to, but I'm too scared. I don't want to sound needy or desperate, plus I'm afraid of what he'll say." She paused for a moment, blowing her nose with a wad of toilet paper. "It's just, I broke up with Matt to be with him, and now Matt's in another relationship, and I'm afraid of getting dumped and feeling humiliated."

"If he does break up with you, there's no reason you should feel humiliated. It would be his loss, right? And even then, would you want to get back together with Matt anyway?"

Paige shrugged. "Probably not. It's just nice to have the security of a boyfriend, and I don't want to lose it. But more importantly, I don't want to lose Tom. I really care about him."

"Look, I'm no expert, but I'm pretty sure relationships aren't supposed to make you feel insecure and scared. I mean, I know they take work and aren't always perfect, but overall, a relationship with someone should make you feel good, right?" I put my arm around her shoulders. "Plus, you would probably find someone new in like ten minutes," I said, trying to sound jovial.

"Are you saying I'm easy?" She raised her eyebrow and frowned at me.

"Noooo, not at all. I'm saying. . . you're Paige Evans. You're beautiful and smart and athletic. Even if you're being super selective, I don't think it will take long for you to find a new boyfriend, if that's what you want to do, and that's if you and Tom even break up." I watched as Paige's mouth shifted to something resembling a smile. "I guess what I'm saying is that you should talk to Tom and get some answers, and try not to worry so much about the possibility of not being with him. You've got lots of other options, one of which is being single. That I am an expert on, and you know, it's really not so bad."

"Really?" She asked as if I had told her chocolate cake doesn't have carbs.

"Really," I said. "I can just do my own thing. I can flirt with someone, make out with someone, maybe feel like a fool the next day when they reject me, and then just move one."

Paige laughed. "You shouldn't feel like a fool. Tristan should feel like an asshole."

"Yeah," I said, shrugging. Enough time had passed since Paige's party for the raw hurt I had experienced the following day to heal. "There are just more important things to worry about, you know?"

"Like what?" asked Paige, sounding skeptical.

"Climate change, poverty, social injustice. Trying to figure out what defines me. I don't know what it is yet, but I'm starting to realize that it's not being someone's girlfriend."

"That's a good point," said Paige. "I guess I need to figure that out too. I mean, I already wrote my essay for Ms. Rose, but I need to figure it out for more than a grade."

"So, what did you write about?"

"Providing medical care," said Paige sniffling and wiping her nose. "When I was in Costa Rica, I volunteered at a hospital. I brought patients their meals, kept the little kids company, and sometimes got to help the nurses with changing bandages and stuff. It's where I met Tom. It changed my life. So now I'm starting to think pretty seriously about medical school."

"That sounds amazing," I said. "And I think you'd be an incredible doctor."

"Thanks. We'll see." Paige stood up from the windowsill and went to look into the mirror above the sink. "I know you think my life is perfect, and it is pretty close to perfect I guess, but it's a lot of pressure, trying to live up to everyone's expectations all the time. I mean, if Tom dumps me, will I still be the it girl of East Point Prep?" She made air quotes when she said 'it'.

I realized then that maybe I had been a part of Paige's problem, always placing her on a pedestal, frequently reminding her how flawless she was. "Paige, you don't have to be perfect, and I'm sorry if I've fed into this idea that you should be. Before we became friends, I always thought you were the opposite of me; graceful, fashionable, admired by all. But now I know you're more than just the stereotypical popular girl. You're caring, you have empathy, you're practical, and you're fun to talk to. Those things aren't going to change if you lose your boyfriend."

Paige leaned in toward me and gave me a hug. "Thanks, Darcy. You're a good friend." It was the first real hug between us, the first time we'd actually put our entire bodies into it. I'd been needing a hug like that from a friend, from someone I could rely on.

"Well, I'm hungry," I said after a moment. "Can we go finish our lunch now?"

Paige nodded. "Do I look like I've been crying?"

I took a dry piece of toilet paper from her hand and wiped the smudge of makeup from under her eyes. "There. You like fine," I said.

"Just fine?" she asked.

"Well, what do you want me to say, perfect?"

"Okay, but seriously. I don't want to go back out there if everyone can tell I've been crying."

"You look normal, not like you've been crying."

We both stood and walked toward the door. As I pushed it open and stepped into the hallway, I nearly collided with Maya, who was just about to enter the bathroom. For a split second we all froze, and my heart might have skipped a few beats. It was the closest I had been to her since Paige's party weeks earlier.

"Excuse us," said Paige, giving me a little push through the doorway.

Maya just stood there silently, looking horrified, like she'd just witnessed a murder, and Paige and I ran back to the cafeteria like we were escaping one. "Well, that was awkward," said Paige when we got back to our table.

"Should I have said something to her?" I asked.

"No. She's the one who owes you an explanation."

"I know. It just feels weird. And honestly, I don't have a crush on Matt anymore anyway, so maybe I should be over it."

"It's not just about Matt. It's about the way she betrayed you. There's no excuse for that."

"Yeah," I said. "I guess that's the way I see it too." I took a bite of my turkey sandwich, despite the sick feeling in my stomach. No matter how much I wanted to agree with Paige, I couldn't help but feel a sense of regret over running from my former best friend. Should I have just said hello like a normal person? Or maybe have used the opportunity to confront her about her actions at the party? I took another large bite of my sandwich, chewing it faster than I could breathe.

"Eating your feelings much?" asked Paige.

"Maybe," I said. "It's either that or bawling in front of everyone in the cafeteria."

Paige put her hand on mine. "Remember what you told me a few minutes ago? Relationships shouldn't make you feel bad. You're better off without friends who treat you like that."

"You're right," I said once I had swallowed my food. Maya returned to her table with Matt and his friends, just two tables away from ours. Had she already known Paige and I were in the bathroom before coming in? From her position she would have seen us get up and leave the cafeteria. But the look of shock on her face was too real. I wondered what was going through her head. Was she angry with me for not returning her calls? Was she embarrassed or remorseful about what had happened and just too stubborn to apologize in person? Did she think that her new relationship was worth losing the friendship she had with me? There were so many questions I had for her about it all, and it seemed like I would never have the answers.

"So, I'm going to take your advice," said Paige, disrupting my thoughts about Maya. "I'm going to call Tom after school and find out what's going on. But if what I'm afraid of happening becomes reality and we break up, I don't want to be alone. Can I do it from your house?"

"Of course," I said. "There's no gardening today, and I'm not cleaning this month, so I'll just be hanging out at home. I haven't been able to do that after school in years."

"Good," said Paige. "You can meet me by my locker after school and I'll drive us to your place. I could really use the girl time."

I looked over at Audrey and Ava, who were both rolling their eyes, but otherwise ignoring our return to the table. "Sounds great," I said, although I wasn't exactly sure what girl time with Paige would even consist of. With Maya it had been laughing about our classmates' self-indulgent and carefully curated Instagram profiles, giving each other quizzes from trashy magazines (yes, the actual printed magazines), watching Trevor Noah on the Daily Show, and ranking how annoying our teachers were. I missed those times with her, just hanging out in one of our bedrooms listening to music and talking, and I hoped that Paige could fulfill the role of best friend as easily as Maya had before she started acting like a stranger.

The bell rang as I finished the last bite of my sandwich. Paige carefully repacked her lunch bag and water bottle. She glanced up at Audrey and Ava, who were already walking away from the table, and gave them a polite wave. While I might not have had much in common with her, I knew I could trust her to be loyal and honest, and aren't those two of the most important qualities in a friend anyway?

"Ready for English?" she asked.

"I'm always ready for a class with Ms. Rose," I said. "Let's go."

ELEVEN

M s. Rose stopped me on the way out the door after class. "How did it go yesterday?" she asked.

"It was amazing," I said. "The kids were great, and I had so much fun."

"I'm so glad to hear that. I knew you'd be a good fit for the gardening program."

"By the way, Mr. Brooks said you should join us sometime," I said.

"I just might do that," she said. From her smirk, I gathered that she and Mr. Brooks had some history between them. As nosey as it was, I couldn't help but wonder if it was romantic. I hoped that it was. Maybe I had a future in match-making. I *had* gotten my former best friend and her boyfriend together without even trying. It must have been a natural talent.

I finished my final two classes and then found Paige, with whom I was acting as more of a match breaker. But even though I knew next to nothing about romantic relationships, I still thought my advice had been solid. Everyone in a relationship deserved clarity. I didn't need to be an expert to know that.

"You ready to go?" I asked.

She slammed her locker shut. "Yep!" she said, with forced excitement. "Let's do this."

We walked down the hallway toward the main stairway. Up ahead I saw Matt and Maya leaning against her locker. She had her back to me and couldn't see me approaching. I decided that if she turned to look at me, I'd take the high road and smile at her. I kept my eyes glued to her back, waiting to make my move, but she never turned around, and so Paige and I just kept walking as if the two of them didn't exist. *Maybe next time*.

Paige and I turned the corner and walked down the stairs. For the first time since starting high school, I was free to do what I wanted. I was one of them, and I was leaving the building with Paige Evans. In a 90s teen movie, I would have been sporting a complete makeover, wearing my hair down and showing off more of my body, but in reality, I didn't look or feel any different. Funny how becoming friends with the popular girl didn't actually require that I change anything about myself.

When we got to the parking lot, Tristan was leaning against his Beemer, presumably waiting for one of his romantic conquests to meet him. He did a double-take as Paige and I approached him. I didn't know if he was surprised to see my leaving school at the regular time or if he was surprised to see me leaving with Paige. Maybe he'd expected her interest in me to fizzle as quickly as his had. I made eye contact with him for a moment, but couldn't decide if I wanted to smile or wave or flip him off or what, so I ended up just staring as Paige and I got into her car.

"He's eyeing you," said Paige. "Too bad he blew it with you already."

"I really doubt he sees it that way."

Paige backed out of her spot and slowly drove past him. He flashed us a cocky nod and smile. "Eww," said Paige. "And if he doesn't see it that way he should. You're way prettier and smarter than the other girls he's been messing around with lately."

"Maybe, but they're cooler than me, and probably more free-spirited."

"I would not call that free-spirited. There's a word for it, but it's not kind so I won't say it."

"You sound like my grandma," I said, laughing. "But I'm glad you're not saying it. It's not cool to slut-shame."

Paige chuckled. "I know right. Like, at some point in recent history, it became worse to slut-shame than it was to act like one. And I know you're a feminist so I wasn't about to go there with you."

"Aren't you a feminist?" I asked, a little worried about what kind of person I was about to engage in girl time with.

"Yeah," she said. "I guess so. I'm just not as outspoken about it as you are."

"Am I outspoken about it?"

"Kind of, but in a good way." Paige had reached the edge of the parking lot and was waiting to turn onto the road. "Remember freshman year, when we were talking about the wage gap in World History?

"Oh yeah, I do."

"Robert Frey made some stupid comment about how men are paid more because they perform better, and corporations only employ women to get them to stop complaining. You straight up went off on him."

"That's right. I totally did. I think I might have nearly blacked out from rage. I don't even remember exactly what I said to him."

"You told him that he makes Neanderthals look advanced, and that the only reason our planet was going up in flames was because men like him had been running it for too long."

"That was as a good burn, if I do say so myself."

"It was epic, and even though I totally agreed with you, I don't know if I would have ever had the guts to tell him off in front of the whole class like that. I was glad you did it though."

I remembered that event with mixed emotions. After I'd unleashed my wrath on Robert, Tristan had said, "Damn," from the back of the room. A few people laughed, and someone even applauded briefly.

Then Robert said, "Don't you have some floors to mop, Darcy?"

"Yes, I do," I'd said, trying hard to maintain my composure. I wasn't going to let him one-up me. "Because unlike you, I work for what I have." I turned back around to face the front of the classroom, eliciting a few more cheers from my classmates, but it stung, knowing that no matter how smart or capable I was, I was seen as the cleaning girl in every class I took at East Point. It made me want to disappear, and it was the last time I ever went out of my way to talk to a classmate, up until I made my deal with Paige. I'd tried to forget it, but knowing that Paige admired me for it made the memory less painful.

"Which way do I go now?" Paige had made her way through the quiet streets that sheltered our school and was nearing the main road.

I directed her to my house until she recognized the streets of my neighborhood. When she parked on my street, she looked around as if she hadn't yet made up her mind about getting out of the car. "We're here," I said. "I know it's not Indian Hill, but I promise you're safe."

"I'm just nervous about calling Tom," she said as she turned off the engine. "But I'm ready now. Let's do it."

We walked into the house and passed through the living room into the kitchen. "I'd give you a tour, but pretty much everything you'd want to see is visible from here so it's not really necessary."

"Where's your room?" she asked.

We walked a few feet down the hallway off the kitchen and through the first door on the left into my bedroom. "This is cute," she said, taking off her backpack and plopping herself down into the cushioned swivel chair that my mom had gotten me for my thirteenth birthday.

"Thanks," I said.

Paige was looking around curiously. After a minute she stood up from the chair to inspect the photos on my dresser. "Is that your mom?" she asked, picking up one of the two of us together. It had been taken by my grandmother in Florida two-and-a-half years earlier. She and my grandpa had rented a beach house for the four us to stay in over my spring break. We had spent most of our time walking up and down the shoreline collecting shells. It was before I'd started school at East Point Prep and hadn't a care in the world. It was the best vacation I'd ever had.

"Yep," I said.

"She's really pretty, and young."

"She's going on forty," I said. "So, I guess she is younger than most other moms we know. She was still in college when I was born, trying to finish nursing school."

"You're like the Gilmore Girls," she said. "Have you ever watched it?"

"Yeah. My mom loves that show. I think she wishes we were more like them."

Paige set the frame down in its spot on my dresser. Her phone started ringing from the side pocket of her backpack. In one swift motion she grabbed it and pulled it out. "It's Tom," she shouted. "He's calling me!"

"That's great," I said. "I'll just step out so you can—"

"Hello," Paige said into her phone, her back turned to me. She sounded calm and casual, not like someone who'd been crying about the person on the other end just hours earlier.

I stepped out of the room, closed the door, and walked into the kitchen. I rummaged through the pantry for a snack, feeling unhopeful since I knew Mom hadn't been grocery shopping in a few days, but managed to find an unopened bag of Quinoa chips, as well as some carrots and ranch dip in the fridge. I pulled my phone out from my sweatshirt pocket, but stopped myself from opening up Instagram or another social media app. I was having a good week, aside from my awkward run-in with Maya, and I didn't want to see or read anything that would spoil it.

Back in junior high, before I had a smart phone, I used to write in my journal almost every day, and now I suddenly had the urge to start it again. Luckily, I'd taken off my backpack in the foyer, so I was able to go get my notebook without interrupting Paige's phone call. I brought my notebook back into the kitchen, flipped to a clean page, and started writing. I reflected on everything that had happened since the start of the school year, starting with Paige's party and all of the highs and lows of the events that followed. I ended the day's entry on a high note, though, describing my time in the garden the day before and meeting a cute guy that I hoped I could maybe become friends with. Yes, it might have been early to mention Sean by name, but there's no point in journaling if you're not going to be honest, and the honest truth was that I'd thought about him more than a couple of times that day.

After about fifteen minutes, Paige emerged from my room, a satisfied smile on her face. "How'd it go?" I asked.

"Great," she said, sitting down next to me at the counter-top. "He actually called to apologize for being so aloof lately. He said he was just feeling overwhelmed with his classes. He thought he was going to flunk out and was afraid to tell me because he thought I'd think less of him, which I told him was ridiculous because I wouldn't lose respect for him over his grades. I mean, he's pre-med, and I know how hard that is. But anyway, he said he's gotten some tutors and his grades are back on track now, so everything's fine. He's even planning to come visit next weekend so he can meet my parents."

"That's wonderful!" I said, leaning in to give her a hug. "I'm happy that you got it resolved."

"Me too," she said. "Sorry for being such a blubbery mess earlier."

"Don't be sorry. I've been a blubbery mess at least a couple of times in the last month. You just haven't had the opportunity to see it yet." I pushed the bag of quinoa chips her way. "Want any?"

"I'll just take a carrot."

I shrugged, reaching into the bag and pulling out a handful.

"Okay, I'll just take a few." She took the bag and pulled out two or three chips, then picked up her phone, opening Instagram. "Don't do it!" I yelled. "I've been trying to stay away."

"Where else am I going to look to find you a boyfriend?" she asked.

"A boyfriend?"

"Yes! Now that my relationship is settled it's time to find one for you."

"I don't know. I'm finally starting to make peace with my life the way it is. I've spent a lot of months wishing for a boyfriend, but now I'm over it."

"Ok then, don't think about it. Let me figure it out for you."

I laughed, nervous to get caught-up in another disappointing and potentially embarrassing romantic pursuit. "I think I learned my lesson after your party. I'd had a crush on Matt, but it turned out that he and Maya had a more natural connection. I think if I ever have a relationship, it should be one that develops naturally."

"Wait," said Paige. She stopped scrolling through the accounts in front of her and looked up toward the ceiling, like she was trying to recall something. "What about that guy that Maya had a thing with before Matt. Nick something. A sophomore, right?"

I was surprised that Paige had even known about that. As it turned out, the popular kids do pay attention to what the outcasts do, they just do a good job of pretending not to. "Nah. That would just seem petty. Plus, I don't think he's my type."

"Ok, then he's out. What about Hollis Schafer? Or Mike Kim? They're both single."

"Really, Paige. You don't need to set me up. First, I need to focus on figuring out myself. Then, maybe I'll try my luck at dating again."

"Do you go to therapy?"

"No. Why?"

"That sort of sounds like something a therapist would tell you to do. I mean, it's good. You should figure out who you are. But there's no reason you can't do that while having a cute guy by your side." Paige clicked her nails on the counter-top, scrunching her eyebrows in contemplation. "What about that guy you mentioned at lunch? The one you met at the gardening club."

"Sean. Yeah, he's nice. I'll see him again tomorrow. But I'm not going to get my hopes up for anything other than friendship with him. That's just a recipe for disappointment."

"What's his last name?" Paige asked, already in the process of searching for him on Instagram.

"I don't know. You're not going to find him. Sean is a fairly common name."

"Where does he go to school?"

"Academy for the Arts."

"Do you know anything else about him?" she asked.

"Hmm, not much. He's a good artist. I saw some of his sketches yesterday."

A minute or so later Paige held her phone out in front of me, a picture of Sean on the screen. "Is that him?" she asked.

"Um, that's a little creepy. How did you find him so fast?"

"You call it creepy. I call it resourceful. I'm good at sleuthing."

"I'll keep that in mind in case I ever need a private investigator. But seriously, how did you do that?"

"Google. There's a photo of him on his school's website. Then I had his full name to find him on Insta. Are these all his drawings?" she asked.

"Yeah. Isn't he good?"

"Really good."

Going through his page, I couldn't help but feel like a peeping Tom. What would he think if he knew my friend was Googling him and tracking down his socials? "Is it weird that we're looking at this?" I asked.

"If he didn't want these photos viewed, he wouldn't have shared them."

"Yeah, but what if he only wants them viewed by certain people?"

"Then he should change his privacy settings."

We continued scrolling, until we got to a picture of him with a red-headed girl. Her face looked familiar. I knew I'd seen her somewhere. After a few seconds of mental searching, I realized that she was the girl that he'd drawn in his sketchbook. "See," I said. "He has a girlfriend. And she's gorgeous. I don't stand a chance, so let's just put the phone away and focus on something else, like my essay. Want to help me brainstorm?"

"Darcy," said Paige reproachfully. "Just relax. First of all, we're just looking at his public photos. There's nothing weird about it. Secondly, we don't know that's his girlfriend. They could just be friends. And even if she is his girlfriend, you can still like him. They're not married or anything."

"I know. I know. I just think it's better if I don't expect anything."

"Okay, so don't expect anything. You could still flirt a little though. It couldn't hurt, right?"

"Ok," I said, hoping to just end the discussion. "I'll try flirting and see what happens." It occurred to me, though, that I didn't exactly know what flirting entailed. I'd only had one romantic interaction, and I didn't really think it involved flirting. We were both drinking and feeling more relaxed because of it. Or had I been flirting a little without realizing it? One of the reasons I'd been so comfortable around Tristan was because he wasn't the guy I was initially trying to impress. Maybe that was why we ended up hitting it off. Maybe I had even been flirting with Sean the day before. I did feel comfortable around him, despite only knowing him for a couple of hours, but I wasn't as confident as Paige. When it came to flirting, I had no idea how to tell whether it was the right amount or over the top. "So, did you have to, um, flirt with Tom when you first started to have feelings for him?" I asked.

Paige smiled, leaning her chin against the palm of her hand. "I don't know if we really flirted exactly. I mean, we were volunteering in a hospital. We were just drawn to each other, so it wasn't really something I made a big effort in trying for. There was never a need to be extra or anything. I just remember smiling whenever he was around because I felt so happy to be near him, and he was always so helpful. If he saw me carrying supplies, he would rush over to help lighten my load. One day I had been volunteering in the nursery of the maternity ward, helping to hold and feed the newborns. There was one baby who'd been born with Neonatal Abstinence Syndrome. She was so small and sweet, and I felt so bad that such a tiny baby could have so many health problems. After I put her down, I went out into the hallway and started crying. Tom walked by and saw me, and he came over and gave me this hug, and he just let me cry on his shoulder for a minute. I felt so secure doing that. I could tell he didn't have an agenda. He just wanted to be there for me, and it felt good."

Paige paused for a moment, then let out a long sigh. I wondered what was going through her mind, if she was thinking about the baby or reminiscing about Tom. "Later that night we were both outside in front of the volunteer housing center and he asked if I wanted to take a walk to the beach with him. So, we just walked, without really saying much, and after a few minutes he started to hold my hand, and it just seemed right. I felt guilty at first because I knew Matt would feel hurt, but I also knew that I had to follow my heart."

I felt like a child being tucked into bed with a story, almost ready to drift off into dreamland, but I needed a complete happy ending to feel satisfied. "So, what about the baby? Will she be ok?"

"I think so, although she'll probably have some developmental issues. The hospital has some really great doctors, though, and I know they'll continue to check in with her. I plan on going back next summer. Maybe I'll even get to see her again if she's still getting treated there."

"You know, Paige, I used to think that all the volunteering in places like Costa Rica mostly consisted of hanging out at the beach, but as it turns out, I was wrong. You did a lot of important work at the hospital. I'm sorry I misjudged you."

"It's ok. I know how the rich kid volunteer storyline comes across." She leaned in toward me and briefly rested her head on my shoulder. We finished the bag of chips, then went to my room to do homework together, but mostly talked instead. We talked about everything; family, what I thought my father might be like, what she thought her half-brother might be like, whether or not civilization would survive another ten years, whether or not we should keep sitting with Audrey and Ava during lunch.

When Mom got home, she looked pleasantly surprised to see Paige in my room with me. She invited her to stay for dinner, but Paige declined, politely. "My dad usually works late," she said, "which means it's just me and my mom for dinner. I probably shouldn't make her eat alone."

"Of course you shouldn't," said my mom, standing in the doorway of my bedroom. "Darcy knows that feeling all too well." Then she smiled and walked into the kitchen, filling up a pot with water to boil for pasta.

Paige packed up her backpack and slung it over one shoulder. "See you tomorrow," she said on her way out of my room. "Nice meeting you, Ms. Walsh," she called out to my mom.

We both said goodbye and watched as she got into her car and drove off. "I'm glad you had a friend over," said Mom. "Did you have a good time?"

"I did," I said. "We did." The afternoon with Paige had been exactly what I'd needed after losing my best friend. It occurred to me as I shut the front door and walked into the kitchen to help with dinner that I officially had a new one.

CHAPTER

TWELVE

The next day at Taft Elementary, I signed in with Mrs. Walker and headed to the cafeteria. Sean was sitting in the same spot as before. I sat down beside him, hopeful that we'd talk while waiting for the kids to come in.

"Welcome back," he said.

"Thanks." I wanted to keep the conversation going, but didn't know what to talk about. I looked around the room, annoyed with myself for not having thought of an interesting question or icebreaker beforehand.

"We're working with the second and third-graders today," he said, saving me the trouble of thinking of something to say.

"Oh. What are they like?"

"They're not quite as sweet and innocent as the younger ones, but they're still pretty good. There are two boys that we have to try to keep separated because they'll end up fighting if they get too close. I'll show you which ones when they come in."

"That's good to know. I'll try to make sure one of them stays with me the whole time."

"That's exactly what I was going to suggest."

"Do you think you could ever be a teacher?" I asked after a brief pause.

"I don't know," said Sean, "I used to think so, but I don't know if I could do what Mr. Brooks does. Some of these kids need so much, and it feels good to help, but I probably wouldn't have the energy to do it all week long."

I nodded. "I don't know if I would either, but wouldn't it be amazing to feel like you were making an impact on them? I mean, teachers literally shape the future."

"It sounds like you might have a teaching career ahead of you," said Sean.

"Maybe," I said. "I don't know what I want to do yet, but teaching could definitely be on the list."

A moment later, the bell rang and the kids streamed through the doors. The balls were bouncing, the sneakers were squeaking, and cartons of milk and fruit cups were being set out on the tables. Mr. Brooks made his announcement to the Junior

Gardeners of the day, and the kids in our group scrambled over to line up behind him. Sean pointed out the two boys that needed to be separated, and I could see why. One was standing behind the other, shoving him from behind, while the one in front made elbow jabs in defense.

"You should take Damien." Sean pointed to the one in the front. "He's the easier of the two."

I tapped Damien on the shoulder to get his attention and introduced myself. "Your friend there is going to walk with Sean," I said. "Would you mind walking with me?" I led Damien away from the other boy, named TJ, making sure at least five or six other kids stood between them.

"He's not my friend," said Damien as we moved back in the line.

"Hmm," I said. "Why don't you and TJ get along?"

"He's always messing with me," said Damien, as the line began moving outside. "I just want him to leave me alone."

I didn't know how to respond at first. I couldn't tell if TJ was a bully and Damien was the innocent victim just trying to stick up for himself, or if there was a different reason TJ singled him out. I didn't know enough about either kid or kids in general to know those answers, nor did I know how to handle the situation long-term. "Just stick with me for today," I said, "I'll make sure TJ doesn't bother you."

Damien looked up at me, sniffling and wiping his nose with his sleeve. I got the feeling that he wanted to trust me, but wasn't totally sure if he could. Something about his stoic demeanor gave me the impression that he was a good kid who was stuck in a difficult situation and used to dealing with it on his own. All I could do on that day was to help him have fun and hope that Sean could keep TJ busy enough to stay away from Damien.

When we arrived at the garden, Damien and the other kids were eager to grab their watering cans and get to work with watering and harvesting the vegetables. This group of kids worked more independently than the littler ones. They knew to water the roots of the plants rather than the tops and to give each plant an equal amount of water. Sean told me that we still couldn't trust them with the sheers, which irritated a few of them, who insisted that they could handle it. From what I could tell, they were probably right, but still, I couldn't risk breaking the rules for anyone.

Only once did TJ and Damien need separating. While waiting in line at the pump to fill his watering can, TJ stuck his foot out in front of Damien, attempting to trip him. Damien kept his balance, but shoved TJ in retaliation. Fortunately, Mr. Brooks witnessed the event and intervened before a bigger brawl could ensue. He pulled TJ aside and made him sit in the gazebo. I ushered Damien back to his plants, and could see that Mr. Brooks had some strong words for TJ, but I wasn't close enough to hear what they were.

Sean, who was standing a few yards away from me, was also observing Mr. Brooks and TJ in the gazebo. Then he looked at me, and for a moment the two of us held eye contact. As if mirroring one another, we simultaneously smiled and waved, which made us both laugh. Behind me some girls giggled. I turned toward them, feeling my cheeks flush.

"What?" I said to them. "We're just saying hi."

They giggled some more. "Let's get back to work," I said. "Those tomatoes aren't going to pick themselves."

TJ came rejoined the group a few minutes later. It seemed like whatever Mr. Brooks had said to him made a profound impact. For the rest of the time in the garden, TJ was on his best behavior, not so much as looking at Damien. After the day's veggies were harvested, the kids brought everything to Mr. Brooks to be washed. Then they enjoyed their salad and pretzel snack while Sean and I leaned against the railing of the gazebo.

"I think we did well today," he said.

"Me too."

He held out his hand in front of me, and I gave him a five. I felt a rush of excitement as my hand touched his, but I tried to act casual about it, like high-fiving cute guys was something I did every day.

"What are you doing after this?" he asked.

I shrugged. "My only plan was to go home and do my homework."

"Well, it is Friday," he said. "Don't you think we should do something fun?"

"Like what?" I asked.

"My parents have this thing they're going to tonight, so they gave me money to order pizza. It's probably enough to order like twelve pizzas though."

"Lucky," I said, trying to sound playful. I wondered if that constituted flirting.

"I know. They do that sometimes. Maybe they feel bad about leaving me alone or something. Anyway, I don't really want pizza, but there is a diner nearby that has a sick all-day breakfast menu. You want to go there with me? It's my treat, obviously."

"Yeah," I said enthusiastically. "I love breakfast food."

"Cool," said Sean.

When the kids were done with their snacks, Sean and I helped Mr. Brooks with cleaning and getting everything prepared for the following week. Then we walked the kids back to school, still making sure to keep Damien and TJ separated, although all the kids were much more peaceful after their time in the garden.

When we arrived at the cafeteria, the kids immediately started running after the dozens of balls that rolled and bounced around. "It's almost time to go home," yelled Mr. Brooks. "Fourth- and fifth-graders, make sure all the balls are put away. Everyone else can help."

Sean and I retrieved our belongings from the corner table. Mr. Brooks turned to address us. "Have a good weekend, you two. Thanks for all your help."

We waved and said goodbye then headed out through the back door. I followed down the sidewalk away from the school. He explained that the diner was about five blocks away from Taft Elementary, and just one block past his school. I texted Mom to let her know I was getting food with a friend and followed Sean away from the elementary school.

"This is it," said Sean, as we walked by The Academy of the Arts. We stopped for a moment to take it in. The building itself was truly a work of art. It was mostly light gray, with windows in alternating shades blue. On the grassy area outside the school were several round, wooden structures, with fence-like bars going all the way around. "What are those for?" I asked.

"They're creative pods," said Sean. "We're allowed to come out and sit in them during our free periods. The idea is that they let you feel connected to the school while still providing security and privacy. At least, that's what the teachers say," said Sean.

"They're amazing," I said.

"We can try one out," said Sean. We walked over to the closest one, and went around to the back side to find the opening. Inside was a circular bench that spanned the inside of the pod. "We probably won't have these much longer," said Sean.

"Why not? They're so cool."

"Kids get busted for smoking in them a lot."

"And that's why we can't have nice things," I said.

"Yep. Nothing good ever lasts," said Sean. We sat there for a bit, observing the sky and building tops through the bars on the pod. Sitting there next to Sean was more calming than anything I'd experienced in a long time. But like Sean said, it probably wouldn't last, and I knew I shouldn't expect it to. After minute we both got up to walk the last block to the diner.

The restaurant had an unassuming exterior, but was completely different on the inside, with the classic black and white tile floor, neon lights stretching along the top of one wall, and a long counter with a row of stools with bright red cushioned seats in front. Sean and I sat down in a booth next to a window overlooking Main Street. "I come here with my friends sometimes after school, on the days I don't have gardening," said Sean.

"Do you have a lot of friends?" I asked.

"I guess." Sean paused and ran his fingers through his hair. "Well, I have a lot of acquaintances, people I see at parties and stuff, but only a few close friends, like people I really trust. What about you?"

"I've got…"—I squinted, crunching up my face—"a friend."

"That's it?" asked Sean. "Is your school that filled with assholes?"

"Well, kind of, but that's only part of the problem. I think the other part is that I'm worried about rejection so I don't really put myself out there."

"Why would people reject friendship with you? I mean, I haven't known you that long, but so far you seem pretty cool."

"Thanks." I shrugged, looking down at the menu, hoping he couldn't tell how self-conscious I was. "I guess I feel like being the school cleaner puts me pretty low in the social hierarchy, so it's easier if I don't really try. It would just lead to disappointment. The last time I put myself out there, I got burned, big time."

"Got burned by who?"

"Just this stupid guy. But he's popular, so it still sucked. And it was at the same time I stopped talking to my former best friend, which made the whole thing worse."

"Well, I don't know this guy, or your former best friend, or any of the details, but if someone passed on a chance with you, I'd say they're an idiot."

"He might not see it that way, but thanks."

Our waitress, an older woman with glasses and a little paper hat, came and took our orders. We each asked for a milkshake, one strawberry and one chocolate. Sean ordered the pancake platter and I ordered the chicken and waffles. We continued talking about friends and school and the difficulty of navigating social situations while trying to stay on top of homework and extracurriculars. I told him about Paige, about how involved she is in student council and running track in the spring, and about how unlikely a friendship with her seemed until recently, given that we'd never actually spoken prior to junior year. I learned that Sean's best friend is a guy named Tyler whom he'd known since elementary school. Tyler went to the same school as Sean, but majored in drama instead of visual art. Sean described him as funny and outgoing. "He's the one who gets all the girls," he said. "And I really do mean *all* the girls, 'cause he doesn't like being tied down to just one."

"I doubt you have that much trouble getting girls either," I said, thinking of the girl I saw in his sketchbook.

"I guess not. I do have those boyish good looks." Sean grinned, showing off his white, perfectly aligned teeth. I couldn't help but laugh at his display of preening.

"Here you go, lovies," said our waitress, handing out our milkshakes and plates of syrup-covered carbs. I immediately got to work, cutting up the chicken, spreading the syrup around evenly.

"Good, right?" asked Sean as I stuffed my face, barely taking the time to breathe.

I nodded, laughing at the realization of how I must have looked. I finished chewing and swallowing the food in my mouth. "I'll have to come here with my mom sometime. She'd love this," I said.

"She sounds cool," said Sean.

"She is. I guess I'm pretty lucky that way."

"What about your dad? Is he cool too?"

I shrugged. "I don't know."

Sean gave me a baffled look. By then, I was feeling comfortable with him, and the tale about my parents just came out without a second thought. I explained it all; my mom's bartending job, the affair with one of her patrons, the brief involvement he had in my life, the decision to remove him from my life so as not to hurt anyone or wreak havoc on another family. Sean sat and took it all in, nodding occasionally to signal his interest in my story.

"I can't believe I told you all that," I said, once I'd finished explaining it all. "That's the second time I've told that story recently, but I don't usually talk about it at all."

"Well, I appreciate being one of the few people you shared it with. That makes me feel special. How does your mom feel about it now?"

"I don't bring it up with her very often. I don't want her to think that I feel like I'm missing out on something, like I'm not grateful for what I already have."

"Do you want to connect with him? I mean, what if he could help you? Maybe he could pay for your school. You wouldn't have to clean anymore. You could keep doing Junior Gardeners with me."

The fact that Sean seemed to want me around more made my cheeks burn. I wondered if he could tell I was blushing. "Paige actually said the same thing, but I'm just not sure I want to. I mean, what if he's broke? What if he's, like, an alcoholic or a drug addict? Or worse, what if he's an asshole? Then I'd just be disappointed."

"Maybe, but then you'd at least know. It's something to think about anyway."

I shrugged. "I'll probably just wait to hear from him. And if I don't, then I guess I'm probably better off without him."

Sean nodded. "Either way, he'd be lucky to have you in his life."

The waitress came by to take our plates, both of which were clean, and dropped off the check. Sean slid the check toward himself and peeked at the total without flipping it over, then put some bills down on top of it. "You ready to go?" he asked.

I nodded. We both stood up and walked outside. It was twilight by then, and the city nightlife scene was coming to life. High heels clicked on the sidewalk and laughter rang through the streets. "They look like they're having fun," said Sean as a group of twenty-somethings in cocktail attire walked past.

"Well, I'm having fun too," I said.

"You are?" he asked, sounding a little surprised.

"Yeah, aren't you?"

He smiled and looked down at his feet. "Yeah, I am," he said. "But I wish we had something else to do. We're too young to go to the bars and clubs down here."

"Just a few more years," I said.

On my left side was a middle-aged man with a briefcase quickly approaching us. "Good evening," he said with a smile, not so subtly staring at me.

"Good evening," I said back as he walked by.

I looked at Sean, whose brow furrowed. "I can't believe how he was looking at you. He's old enough to be our dad."

I laughed, trying to make how awkward I felt. "He wasn't that old, was he?"

Sean nodded and laughed as we stepped away from the restaurant and started walking toward the park. As we got closer, we noticed a crowd forming around a stage on the center of the green. "Oh yeah," said Sean. "They're doing free concerts in the park every Friday night this month. You wanna check it out?"

"Yes!"

We headed over toward the congregation of people. As we waited for the music to start more and more people began to crowd around. The energy and anticipation rose as the sun continued to set. I looked over at Sean, and had the sudden realization that I'd never been to a concert before. My limbs tingled with the realization that I was experiencing this milestone with him. "Sean," I said, "this is my first concert."

"For real?" he said.

I nodded. The loud sound of audio feedback from the stage made us both jump, and after a quick and inaudible introduction, a band consisting of a drummer, a guitarist, and bass player was in full throttle. We both covered our ears, laughing. Then the vocalist came in, whining incomprehensibly into the microphone. We looked at each other in confusion. The feedback continued alongside the cacophony of instruments and screeching vocals.

"This band might suck," said Sean, putting his mouth up to my ear.

"They definitely suck," I said.

"Do you want to get out of here?"

I nodded, and we both pushed our way through the crowd, running for the sidewalk like scared animals escaping a predator. Once we made it out safely, we both doubled over in laughter. "I'm sorry your first concert was so terrible," said Sean, panting a bit.

"It's ok. I guess if you want a good concert you have to pay."

"But I thought all the best things in life were free."

"There's an asterisk. Live music performances don't apply." We started walking down the sidewalk toward the other end of the park. "Actually, you're right about the best things in life being free," I said. "The band sucked, but I still had fun with you, which makes up for the crappy music."

"I had fun with you too." Sean looked down at his feet at first, but then he looked up at my face with a warm, closed-lip smile. We kept walking until we found a bench near the outskirts of the park. It was fully dark by then. Traffic lights and headlights twinkled along both ends of the block. "Should we head to our bus stop?" I asked.

"The busses aren't running too often this late in the evening, but I can get us an Uber." Sean held out his phone, showing me his Uber app.

"You have an Uber account?"

"My dad set one up for me a while ago, in case of emergencies. He knows public transportation isn't always reliable. I've only used it once, so I think he'll be cool with me using it tonight."

I watched as he prepared to find us a ride. "I'll have the driver drop you off first. What's your address?"

I took his phone and typed it in for him, then handed back the phone so Sean could complete the request. A few seconds later an alert popped up, telling him 'Brian' was on his way to pick us up. He appeared to be a young guy with dirty-blonde hair and glasses. "Brian looks all right," said Sean.

"Thank you for doing all this for me," I said.

"It's not a lot. I dragged you out here to hang out with me, so the least I can do is make sure you get home safe."

Brian arrived within a few minutes, driving a silver SUV. When we got in the car, country music played softly from the speakers. I usually hated country music, but this song wasn't so bad, and I had a feeling that I would think of this night if I ever heard it again.

"Are you on Instagram?" asked Sean once the car was moving. He had the app open in front of him.

"Yeah, although I've been trying to stay off it." I took his phone from him, typing my username into the search bar to bring up my profile.

"Why's that?" he asked, clicking on the follow button on my profile.

"I don't like constantly comparing myself to other people. It makes me feel lame."

"I get what you mean," said Sean. "I like your profile picture, though. It's cute."

It was a picture that Maya had taken of me over the summer. We were at King's Island, a nearby amusement Park. I was standing in front of the mini-Eiffel Tower, making a peace sign, and puckering my lips. I was wearing sunglasses, a striped shirt, and short denim shorts, my hair pulled up on the top of my head with a scrunchie. *Say VSCO girl*, I remember Maya saying when she took the photo. I laughed, realizing I had mostly unintentionally been rocking that look.

"Thanks," I said, taking out my phone to follow him back.

Sean tucked his phone back inside his pocket. "I can see why you'd want to stay away from it. It can be toxic at times. But personally, I view it as my public art portfolio. It might seem silly, but I kind of hope to make a name for myself as an artist someday."

"I don't think it's silly at all. You're really talented. And that's a great way to get your name out there."

"We'll see," he said.

I held his gaze for a moment before looking out the window, taking in the city lights until our driver exited the highway and entered my neighborhood.

"Here we are," I said, "the scenic Norwood."

"Cut your 'hood a break," said Sean, picking up on the sarcasm in my voice. "Norwood's got some good spots. I mean Rookwood Commons? That's pretty swanky. You've even got a Whole Foods there."

"Yeah, I guess it's not too bad. And at least it's close to everything."

Brian took a right turn off the main road, nearing my street. I was exhausted, but also the happiest I'd been in years, like a child who'd spent the day roaming the zoo or splashing in the ocean. I'd only known Sean for a couple of days, and yet I couldn't help but feel like we had a connection. But after what happened with Tristan, it was hard to trust my intuition. I wouldn't let myself get carried away. I would live in the moment and enjoy what was happening without any expectations for the future.

"This is me," I announced, as Brian pulled up to my house. "Thanks for everything tonight, Sean. See you Monday?"

Sean nodded. "Good night, Darcy."

I went inside and walked into the kitchen. On the counter were two twenty-dollar bills and a note from my mom that read:

> *Darcy, I figured that if you were going out with a friend,*
> *then I should too. Grabbing drinks with a co-worker. Won't*
> *be out very late. Here's some money to order pizza if you're*
> *still hungry when you get home.*

It was the perfect conclusion to the evening, knowing that my mother was out enjoying herself. I left the money where it was and retreated to my bedroom, eager to get to work on my journal entry for the day. I had a lot to write about.

THIRTEEN

On Monday morning I got to school early after making a Starbucks run with my mom. It was a warm day, so I drank my mocha outside in the courtyard. I was pouring over my chemistry notes in preparation for the quiz later on, when a large figure appeared next to me. When I looked over, there was Matt Holmes, just inches away from me. I jumped up a bit, splashing my mocha onto my uniform skirt and notebook.

"I'm sorry," said Matt. "I didn't mean to startle you."

"It's ok," I said, rummaging through my backpack in search of a napkin or tissue to clean the spill.

"Here," said Matt, handing me a wet nap. "I got wings after football practice last week, so I have a bunch of them if you need more."

"I'm good." I wiped off my skirt and sat back down on the bench, clearing my throat. Never in my life had I sat so close to Matt Holmes. A year earlier I would have swooned, but now I was just flustered, confused, and slightly irritated. "Is there something you need?"

"Yeah, I've been wanting to talk to you for a while, but it seems like every time I see you, you're with Paige. I thought now would be a good time since you're alone."

"Ok." I closed my notebook and put it away. Clearly, he wanted to discuss something personal.

"So, I don't know if you realize this, but Maya feels really bad about what happened at Paige's house last month. She told me about the situation with you and how you had feelings for me, which I never would have known by the way, and how you wouldn't call her back afterward."

Reliving that night in my mind made my cheeks burn. The feeling of uselessness during our three-way discussion, the sight of the two of them kissing in a hidden corner. And now, here was Matt, acknowledging his understanding of the embarrassment I'd felt, which I'd hoped to keep hidden from him. But of course Maya would tell him about why our friendship had deteriorated. I shouldn't have been surprised. "I don't have those feelings for you anymore," I said, although now that he was right next to me, it was hard to deny that there might still have been some attraction. "It was just a crush. I'm over it."

Matt nodded. "Anyway, Maya's been acting different lately. She seems kind of depressed, more withdrawn. I think she feels guilty about the way things worked out. She didn't mean to hurt you. The thing between us just happened. It wasn't planned at all. I think we were both really surprised by how fast we clicked. And now, I think she really misses her best friend."

"You mean me?" I asked with a scoff.

"Of course, you," he said. "Before you guys were practically inseparable."

"If she misses me then why doesn't she just come talk to me?"

"Because she's scared," he said. "She's afraid you'll reject her, yell at her, cuss her out in front of the whole school."

For a moment I just sat there, staring at the Starbucks cup in my hand, twirling it around, unsure of what to say or how to feel. "Did she ask you to talk to me?" I finally asked.

"No. She has no idea I'm doing this."

"I miss her too," I said. "But I've been waiting for her to apologize to me. And I'm not mad at her for dating you. I'm mad, or was mad, because she did something that she knew would hurt me behind my back, without talking to me about it first. I just didn't think she was capable of that."

I looked over at Matt. He was looking down at his knees. A lock of his hair hung down, obscuring his eye. I remembered looking at him in the hallway on the first day of school, seeing that lock of hair over his eye and wanting to stroke it back. For a second, I put my hand out, ready to go for it, but then quickly put it back on my lap, hoping he didn't notice the movement. I wasn't his girlfriend. I never would be, and that was for the best.

"I know you were hurt, but just think about it," he said. "I think Maya really needs you right now."

"I won't yell at her or cuss her out," I said, standing up and slinging my backpack over my shoulder. "But if she wants me to consider forgiving her, she needs to make the first move. You should tell her that." I turned away and started walking toward the school entrance.

"Darcy," called Matt. I turned and faced him again. "Would you give Tristan another chance?"

"Another chance at what?" I asked.

"I don't know exactly. Dating? Hanging out?"

I laughed. "I don't know what he told you, but he's the one who rejected me. Paige's party was just full of delights."

Matt shrugged. "I'm pretty sure he regrets that now. The thing is, he was kind of already involved with another girl when that happened. He didn't really think they were exclusive, but apparently that was how she viewed it, so he was trying to do right by her. But now they're broken up, and he's open to dating other people again. He didn't like hurting your feelings. I know that for a fact."

"Well, I'll believe it when I hear it from him. And what are you anyway? The assholes of East Point PR rep?" I didn't wait to hear his reaction, and instead turned to walk inside, this time without turning back. I felt a sense of victory as I walked the halls toward homeroom, but my heart still pounded in my chest and my arms were shaky, as if I'd just left a high-stress job interview. The fact that I'd just discussed some of my most intimate feelings with someone I barely knew and had always admired from afar was surreal, and nerve-wracking. At least I'd kept my pride and composure.

I went to the back row of seats as usual, walking by Tristan, who gave me a coy wave that I acknowledged with a slight tilt of my head. I wondered if Matt was right about him feeling bad for blowing me off. Chances were, he'd just burned his bridges with every other girl in school and no one left to turn to. I had to admit, there was something about his goofy and often cocky demeanor that I felt oddly infatuated with. What was it about the bad boys that always had the good girls like me so hooked? This isn't *Grease*, I told myself, and you're not Olivia Newton John. After sitting down, I returned to my chemistry notes. Saponification was more important than the motivations of either Matt or Tristan, at least for now.

"Hey girl," said Paige, sitting down next to me, removing her ear buds.

"Hey," I said.

I'd had a good weekend. I was relaxed and ready for my chemistry quiz. I was sitting next to my best friend. Everything was as it should have been, but still, I couldn't help feeling off.

...

During lunch, I filled Paige in on the conversation I'd had with Matt. We'd diverted from the usual seating arrangement and were sitting at a small round table in the far corner of the cafeteria, far from any other parties involved.

"Were you surprised that he came to you?" she asked, pushing around her salad with her fork.

"Yes! When I saw him, I jumped up and spilled my coffee like an idiot." I scooted my chair closer to her and pointed out the stain on my skirt.

"That should come out," she said, running her fingers across it. "Just spray some Shout on it before you put it in the wash."

"Paige, I'm not worried about the stain. What do you think I should do?"

"About Maya?"

"Well, yeah."

"It sounds like she wants you to feel guilty now, even though she's the one who tossed your friendship away after being left alone with a cute boy for like ten minutes."

"Yes, you have a point, but Matt said Maya didn't know he was talking to me. I don't think it was about guilt. I think he's just worried about her. I want her to know that she screwed up, but I don't know if I want her feeling depressed."

Paige sighed and took bite of her salad. "It's your call, Darcy," she said after swallowing. "If it were me, I'd stand my ground, but maybe I'm a cold-hearted bitch."

"You're not a cold-hearted bitch."

Paige shrugged. "I have my moments, but this isn't about me. You have to decide what you want, and if that's forgiving Maya, then I'll support you on that."

"Thanks," I said. I still wasn't sure how I would handle the situation, but I was relieved to know that Paige wouldn't judge me for extending the olive branch. The thought of losing another close friend was scarier than the thought of being rejected by every guy in the school.

"But if you and Maya get close again, just promise you won't ditch me, ok?"

"Paige." I leaned in and gave her a quick hug, knowing she didn't like them to linger too long. "You've become my best friend over the last few weeks. If Maya and I do become friends again, it isn't going to change us."

"Good," said Paige with a smirk. "Because I really don't want to go back to sitting with those bitches." She gestured toward a table behind us, and I didn't have to turn around to see who they were.

I smiled, taking a huge bite of Paige's salad and shoving it into my mouth.

"Hey," she yelled.

"Well, you're not eating it," I said with my mouth full.

"We still have three minutes."

"Then eat it," I said, handing her the fork.

"You better not be sick." She stabbed the largest chunk of lettuce, smothered it in dressing and cheese, and crammed it into her mouth.

"Yes! I've been dying to see you eat like an actual human."

Paige rolled her eyes. "You gave me no choice."

"That's why I'm your best friend." I finished the last bite of my chicken salad sandwich and crumpled up the paper. I watched Paige eat her salad more heartily than before, basking in the gratification of how far I'd come thus far in my junior year. A few weeks ago, it had taken all of my courage to strike up a conversation with Paige after English class, and now here we were, eating lunch together like a couple of old ladies who'd known each other for years. If I hadn't offered to clean up after her party then I might not have lost my friendship with Maya or become entangled with Tristan, but I also wouldn't have become friends with Paige. With Paige, I was more confident. She'd convinced me that I could achieve whatever I wanted to work toward, that I was worthy of it. With me, she was more relaxed, less focused on reputation, and freer to be herself. It was a match made in friendship heaven, and one that I wouldn't let go of easily.

"Shall we go discuss some Julia Alvarez?" asked Paige, standing up with her tray.

"I thought you'd never ask."

...

After school ended, I went to my locker to collect the books I needed for homework. At the other end of the hall, Paige walked toward the West Wing stairwell doors. "Bye, Darce," she yelled. I blew her a kiss, then shut and locked my locker.

I turned to the other side, where Maya and Matt stood by his locker. Matt looked up and met my gaze. Then he leaned in toward Maya, whispered something into her ear and gave her a kiss on the cheek before turning toward the main staircase. Maya turned to face me. She looked worried, like she'd just been told she was about to take the SATS without any time to prepare. I walked toward her, stopping about an arm's length away. She looked at me, then looked down at her feet. But I'd taken the step to walk over, and there was no way I was going to talk first. I pursed my lips, lightly tapping my foot, waiting for her to say something, anything.

"Hi," she said after a moment.

"Hi," I said. Now we were getting somewhere.

"Darcy," she said after another pause. "I'm sorry about what happened at the party. And I'm sorry we've gone so long without talking. This"—she moved her hands out toward me and then back to her chest—"shouldn't be so hard."

"I know," I said. "And I forgive you." She looked up at me, her face softening in relief. "And I want you to know that I don't have feelings for Matt anymore. I think it was just a phase I needed to grow out of. I'm just hurt that you had no reservations about kissing a guy you knew I liked, after telling me that I should take a chance with him. It felt so humiliating."

"I know. I know," said Maya, looking at her feet again. "Believe me, I wasn't planning on it. It all just happened so fast. He wanted to show me the wine cellar, because it was quieter in there, and we were having a difficult time hearing each other with all the noise around us, but I swear I didn't plan on doing anything like that. It just happened, and honestly, I don't think those wine coolers helped one bit." She smirked. I knew that she had meant for that last part to be funny, but I wasn't quite ready to laugh with her yet. "When you didn't return my calls, I assumed that you didn't want to talk to me, so I just left it at that, but I should've sucked it up and apologized in person."

"Yeah," I said. "You should have." I had ten minutes before I needed to catch my bus for Gardening Club. There was still so much to say, so much to figure out, but it would have to wait.

"I'm sorry," she looked back up at me. "I just hope that we can become friends again. Even if I'm just like a side friend and not a best friend, I'll take what I can get."

I chuckled in spite of myself. "I hope so to."

"So, I noticed you're not cleaning after school anymore."

I nodded. "I got a new gig, gardening with elementary kids. But it's temporary."

"That sounds really cool. I'm glad you get to have some fun for a change."

"Yeah. It is fun." I took my phone out of my sweatshirt pocket to check the time, a bad habit I indulged in about every minute when I was anxious or nervous about being late. I'd just received a message from Sean. *Looking cloudy. Hope we don't get rained out.*

I smiled, excited that he had texted, even if it was with bad news. I wondered if he was disappointed by the prospects of not seeing me. I could only hope that the weather would hold out. I looked up at Maya, who was looking at me expectantly. "I actually need to get going now," I said. "My bus is coming soon."

"Oh," said Maya. She sounded disappointed, like she'd thought our conversation was going to continue as we left school together.

"We'll talk again soon," I said. I started to walk away, then turned around, wanting to leave the conversation on a positive note. "And by the way, you and Matt do seem like a good couple, so I think everything turned out the way it was supposed to."

"Thanks," she said with a smile. She tucked her wavy hair behind her right ear and slammed her locker shut. "I'm glad we squashed our beef."

"Me too," I said. I breathed a sigh of relief, the kind you experience after completing a daunting task that you've imagined as unbearable. Write book report for German: Check! Make up with Maya: Check! It had been doable, and maybe even slightly enjoyable. Our joint account of trust might have been depleted, and I knew that she would need to make a shit ton of deposits to restore it, but I also knew that I never wanted to let a crush on a boy come between me and a close friend again. Ever.

I rushed down the stairwell and outside through the main doors. The clouds that Sean had mentioned were dark and foreboding, looking like they would unleash their wrath at any second. Thunder rumbled somewhere in the distance. But just behind the clouds were rays of sunshine, pushing back like those dependable superheroes in every action movie ever made. I grabbed my phone to reply to Sean. *I think we're good.*

CHAPTER

FOURTEEN

"Today is the day, Darcy," said Ms. Rose. English class had just ended and I was packing up my bag and waving to Paige, who was already darting off to her next period.

The day happened to be our last day of Junior Gardener's Club. The plants had pretty much all been harvested, and our first freeze of the season would be coming any day. Is that what Ms. Rose was referring to? Then I remembered the message from Mr. Brooks that I'd given to her after my first day. "You're coming?" I exclaimed.

Ms. Rose nodded, holding up a black gym bag. "I've got my sneakers and outdoor work clothes in here. Would you like to ride over with me?"

I hesitated. Ms. Rose was my favorite teacher, but the thought of a twenty-minute car ride with her seemed intimidating. What would we talk about? Would she grill me on my interpretation of *The Bean Trees*? (Which I had been enjoying but didn't want to be quizzed on before having more time to reflect on the important passages that I'd highlighted.) Would she attempt a casual conversation about art or politics that I wouldn't be able to keep up with because I wasn't cultured enough? Ultimately, I knew it would be rude not to accept her offer without a valid reason. "Sure," I said, my voice wavering. "That would be great."

"Great!" she said. "I'm so excited!" But something about her face made me question the veracity of that statement. She shoved the gym bag under her desk and placed her hands on her hips, blowing a piece of hair out of her eyes with a large breath.

I looked at her in confusion, wondering if I should say anything else before awkwardly leaving the room, until she spoke again. "Actually, I'm pretty nervous," she said, biting her bottom lip. "I really don't know anything about gardening, and I'm used to teenagers, not little kids. But you'll be there, and you can show me the ropes, right?"

"Right!" I said quickly, eager to reassure her. "The kids are great. They'll love you. And the gardening stuff is pretty simple. Today's actually the last day in the garden until spring, so we'll mostly just be preparing everything for winter. Pulling out the plants, putting them into compost, cleaning up and gathering all the supplies."

"Ok" she said, relaxing her stance a little. "I think I can handle that."

Still, there was a look of apprehension on her face. Students from the next period were coming into the classroom, and I was starting to find myself in the way as they moved around me to get to their desks. "It'll be fun," I said, inching toward the door. "I'm really stoked that you're coming."

"That's just what I needed to hear."

"See you soon," I said as I stepped out of the classroom.

"Meet me in the faculty parking lot after school," she called out. I poked my head back inside and gave a thumbs-up to confirm our plan, then dashed down the hall for German.

I sat down in my usual spot, right in the middle of the class-room. Matt, who was sitting a couple of rows over from me, was chatting with a girl named Gabby, who sat in the seat next to him. Was he flirting with her? I decided not to worry about it. *He is allowed to talk to people.* A relationship in which the parties felt like they couldn't talk to other people didn't sound like a healthy one anyway. In the minute before class started, I took my phone out from the front pocket of my backpack and texted Sean. *My English teacher is coming today!*

...

I found Ms. Rose leaning against her sage green Prius. She had already changed into her gardening clothes: a pair of khaki colored- cargo pants with elastic ankles and a dark green T-shirt. I, too, had changed into my black yoga pants, grey T-shirt and dark blue zip-up hoodie. "I love your car," I said.

"Thanks," she said, opening her door. "It's a plug-in hybrid. Hop on in."

Ms. Rose docked her phone and opened up her GPS. "I hope parking won't be too arduous down there."

"I don't drive, but I have noticed spots near the school before, so I don't think you'll have a problem."

"Oh, great." She looked over at me and smiled. "So, you normally take a bus?"

"Yep. It's not bad, but riding with you is obviously superior."

Ms. Rose giggled. "Well, you haven't seen my driving yet."

"Oh," I said, laughing nervously.

"I'm teasing," she said after letting her joke sink in for a moment. "I actually have an impeccable driving record. Never been in an accident. Never gotten a ticket. You're in good hands."

"Isn't that the slogan of one of those insurance companies? You could be their spokesperson."

"Hmmm," she said. "Would I be the insurer or the insured?"

I thought for a moment, trying to come up with a witty reply, but didn't get anywhere. "You could probably do both," I said, finally.

Surprisingly, Ms. Rose laughed, a real laugh. I loosened up some, feeling more at ease. Talking to Ms. Rose was less intimidating than I'd expected. Much to my relief, there was no discussion of class related topics on the way to the school. Instead, Ms. Rose asked me to tell her about how the volunteer job was going. I told her all about it: the puppy-dog like kindergarteners and first-graders, the less innocent but still mostly sweet second- and third-graders, and the too-cool-for-school fourth- and fifth-graders, who enjoyed gardening more than they wanted to let on. I told her about helping the little ones with the watering and harvesting, and about providing encouragement and support to the older ones, and about the importance of getting them to talk to you, asking them about their day and listening to their stories of trouble at school or at home. I told her about making sure they all have the chance to eat a healthy snack, even if there wasn't that much to harvest from the garden (Mr. Brooks always had back-up food), since some of the kids really relied on meals they get from school. I also told her about how awesome Mr. Brooks was, and about how effortless he made his job look, and how all the kids, even the 'bad ones,' generally respected his authority without too much opposition.

"Yeah, he has that effect on people," said Ms. Rose. "I did some student teaching with him a while back, when we were both just finishing our degrees. It was middle school, probably the most difficult age group for teachers, but Mr. Brooks handled it so well. I could tell then that he was going to be a phenomenal teacher."

Ms. Rose was approaching the school. "There's a spot," I said, pointing to an open space on the street on the side of the building near the lunchroom doors. There were so many questions I wanted to ask her about Mr. Brooks, but I stifled my curiosity, or really nosiness, knowing I couldn't pry into the private life of my teacher.

We stepped out of the car and I led the way toward the front of the building, where we both signed in with Mrs. Walker. "Lovely to see you, Darcy," she said as we approached her desk. "And you must be Ms. Rose."

"I am." Ms. Rose signed her name in the guestbook and handed it back to Mrs. Walker.

"I've heard a lot of great things about you from Mr. Brooks." Mrs. Walker looked around, presumably to make sure no one else was in ear-shot, and leaned in toward Ms. Rose. "Now, he wouldn't want me telling you this, but I've never seen Mr. Brooks more concerned about impressing somebody as he was about impressing you. He wanted everything to be perfect for you today."

"Really?" said Ms. Rose. I looked over at her to see her cheeks flush, an embarrassed-looking expression on her face. "That doesn't sound like him."

"Trust me," said Mrs. Walker. "I've known him a long time, and he's been acting different all day. He told me to keep an eye out for you at least three times, so I know something's up."

"He knows I can be directionally challenged," said Ms. Rose. "He probably just didn't want me getting lost in here." She took a backward step toward the door.

"Bye, Mrs. Walker," I said, trying to give Ms. Rose, who was visibly flustered, an easier out. "Have a great weekend!"

I led us down the hall and to the cafeteria, pointing out the best art projects along the way. This time, since our method of transportation had been more direct than the bus, we arrived just before Sean, who usually beat me by at least ten minutes. I introduced him to Ms. Rose, who immediately jumped into what seemed like a casual interview with him, asking him about where he went to school and upon hearing the name of his school, what he specialized in. He told her about his drawing, and at her behest took out his sketchbook. I was sitting in the middle, so I stood up and moved to the other side of Sean, giving Ms. Rose a better look. I watched as he flipped through it with her, taking note of the newest ones; a man and a young boy sitting on the stoop of a rowhouse, a row of vendors at a farmer's market, and then one of what looked like a teenage girl bending down to pick something from a plant within a garden. I looked at it for a moment, registering that there was something familiar about it. Then I realized that it was a drawing of me. I wanted to squeal out loud, but kept the excitement hidden as well as I could.

"That's so lovely," said Ms. Rose. "That girl kind of looks like Darcy. Oh, wait." She looked over at me and then back at the drawing.

"Yeah, it is," said Sean, matter-of-factly. I wanted to react the right way, but it was hard to know whether or not he'd even wanted me to see it. I couldn't tell if he was embarrassed or proud to show it to us. If I could have seen his face, I would have been able to gauge his feelings, but he was looking down at his notebook, and I couldn't see his expression.

"It's beautiful," I said. Even from a totally objective standpoint, the drawing was exquisite.

"Thanks," he said, turning his head toward me slightly, but not enough for me to get a good read of his facial expression. He closed his book and slid it back into his backpack. Ms. Rose put her hands on her heart and looked over at me with an adoring expression, as if to say, *Isn't that so sweet?* I smiled and shrugged a little, hoping to convey that I liked the picture but didn't want to make a huge deal out of it, even though it felt like a freaking huge deal.

A few seconds later the bell rang, making Ms. Rose jump a little. Almost immediately Mr. Brooks came in, followed by the gym teacher, and the gaggle of afterschool students. "Ms. Rose!" shouted Mr. Brooks, clapping his hands as he said her name. Ms. Rose stood and took a step or two forward, but Mr. Brooks practically ran to her, leaning in to give her a hug before she could go any farther. "It's great to see you," he said.

Sean finally turned to face me, raising an eyebrow. I nodded, holding back laughter, silently answering his silent question. *Yes, he definitely likes her.*

Mr. Brooks called out to the Junior Gardeners of the day: the second- and third-graders. Ms. Rose stood next to him at the front of the line. The kids marveled over her, many of them clamoring to find out who she was and if she was a new teacher at the school. She smiled, waved, and held her index finger up to her lips, trying to help calm the chaos. Mr. Brooks announced her as his very special guest who was helping for the day, and instructed the kids to treat her with even more respect than they gave to him.

"See you over there," said Sean as we both rose from the bench and walked down toward the line of children. As usual, he walked alongside TJ in the front of the line and I stood next to Damien in the middle. We had been successful in keeping the two boys separated over the last couple of weeks, and things had been peaceful, at least during the short time spent in the garden, but Damien still seemed sullen and irritable. I suspected that something else was going on with him, and hoped that I could chip away at the dam that was holding back his stifled emotions and get him to open up a little. Maybe there wouldn't be anything I could do to help him, but then again, maybe there would be.

"How was school today, Damien?" I asked as we stepped outside.

Damien shrugged. "I don't really like school." He was looking down at his feet as we walked, kicking at all the little pebbles and bits of debris on the sidewalk.

"Oh," I said. "Why is that?"

"Last week, Chloe said no one likes me."

My heart sank. Damien was a sensitive kid, and already, in second-grade, he was dealing with cliques and rejection from classmates. I knew what it felt like to feel unappreciated, unnoticed, and even disliked, ever since the fourth-grade when I'd been informed by a former friend that she wasn't going to play with me at recess anymore because I was the least cool girl in all of the fourth-grade classes combined. I guess I'd always carried that baggage with me, and I knew how devastating it could be to hear news like that from a peer.

"Well Chloe's wrong," I said firmly. "Because I like you, and I know Sean does too."

"But you and Sean are teenagers," he said, as if teenagers were criminals or something else inherently bad. "That means you're almost grownups."

"That's true, we are a little older, and I know it's important to have friends your own age, but I still know that Chloe was wrong." I reflected on all the wisdom I'd received over the years regarding mean girls and bullies, and remembered something my mom had said to me after I'd told her about becoming the least cool girl. "Sometimes kids will say things like that when they're going through a hard time. Maybe Chloe isn't feeling good about herself right now, and she thought that by saying something mean to you she might feel better somehow, like more powerful or something. But that doesn't make it ok, and it definitely doesn't make it true."

Damien didn't look convinced, but then I didn't always accept my mom's advice about social dilemmas either, at least not right away. Some lessons have to be learned over time. "I don't think Chloe feels bad about herself. She seems like she really likes herself, like she thinks she's the best at everything." I knew what he meant about Chloe. She was a petite girl who exuded confidence and authority. While I hadn't personally heard her degrade another student to the extent Damien had described, I had noticed her tendency to control the kids around her in the garden, giving them orders as effectively as one of the teachers, telling the other kids to fill her watering can or telling them they were doing something the wrong way. "Lucy," I once whispered after hearing Chloe give her an order of some kind, "you don't have to do what she says. She can do it herself."

"It's ok," Lucy had replied. "I don't mind doing it."

I guess that was just the effect that Chloe had on the other kids, and maybe she was a natural born leader. But I didn't know why she would transition from bossing her friends around to straight-up bullying them.

We had arrived at the garden, and everyone was filing through the gate. I bent down a little before going in so I could speak to Damien at his level. "I don't know why she said that, but I can promise you it isn't true. I know that making friends can be hard. It wasn't always easy for me either, but hang in there, Damien. Just remember to keep your head up. Once you get good at being friends with yourself, it will be easier to make friends with other people."

"I should be friends with myself?" he asked.

"Yep. As weird as it sounds, it's actually really important. It's something I've been working on too, for myself."

"How do you do it?"

"Well, you spend time doing the things that you like doing, even if there's no one else around to them with you. You ignore the voices in your head that say negative things. Like sometimes, I hear voices in my head saying that I'm not as smart or as cool as the other people around me, but now I know to ignore them, and replace them with my own voice. I remind myself that I *am* smart, and that I'm good at a lot of things. And you know what? Being here in the garden with you and the other kids from Taft has made me a lot better at doing that."

"Really?" asked Damien. I knew that there was a chance my advice was going over his head, but he was looking more calm than he did a few minutes earlier, so I hoped I was reaching him, at least a little bit.

"Really. And I know it might take some time, but eventually you'll find something that you really like and you're good at too. But in the meantime, just keep your head up. Don't listen to the people who try to make you feel bad. They don't know as much as they think they do, ok?"

"Ok," he said finally.

"Are you ready to go in now?" I asked.

He nodded, and I reopened the gate, letting him step into the garden before me. Sean was in the far-right corner, gathering some spades from the shed, and Mr. Brooks was showing Ms. Rose around the garden, walking up and down the rows of plants, many of which had already been pulled and added to compost. Judging by their expressions, she was impressed with how he had designed and built the space, and he was proud to show it off to her. If we had been in a romantic comedy, audiences everywhere would be rooting for the two of them to finally fall in love and get married after overcoming a decade of hurdles, misunderstandings and missed opportunities. Maybe things would actually work out for the two of them. Or maybe they were just friends and I needed to mind my business, but that wasn't as much fun.

I walked over to Sean and took a few spades from him to give out to the kids. I noticed Damien standing next to Lucy. Chloe was in the same row, but a couple of kids stood in between her and Damien. I thought that maybe I could encourage some camaraderie between Damien and Lucy. If the two of them teamed up, Chloe might not have as much influence over them. "Hey you guys," I said, handing each of them a spade. "Do the two of you want to work on digging up those tomato plants there?" They both nodded. Lucy skipped off to the other side of the garden, Damien scurrying behind her. Lucy was talking, excitedly bobbing her head around as she spoke, while Damien listened, shoving his spade into the soil, a look of contentment on his face. *Job well done*, I told myself.

I looked around at the sea of children dancing and running around. With most of the vegetable plants already fully harvested or pulled out, there was little work to be done, aside from covering the garden beds in mulch to enrich the soil for the spring. I turned to see Mr. Brooks and Ms. Rose opening the mulch bags and emptying them into a wheelbarrow. Once all the plants were pulled out, they walked around and scooped the mulch out with a shovel, spreading it over the soil in each raised bed. Ms. Rose looked slightly awkward as she moved the shovel, leading me to think she hadn't done much yard work before, but she looked happy just the same.

Sean and I each grabbed a shovel to help with spreading the mulch. Five weeks ago, I hadn't even known that this garden existed, and since then it had become integral to my sense of belonging. East Point Prep could go on without me if I suddenly stopped showing up. Mrs. Masterson might offer my cleaning discount to another student, or maybe just hire another janitor. My friends would make other friends and would maybe try to keep in touch, but also maybe not. My life might be in shambles, but everyone else would be just fine. But these kids would miss me. And the garden; it needed me. Or maybe I was the one who needed it. Either way, I dreaded the thought of returning to my cleaning duties the following Monday. If only I could keep this going, I thought, I'd find another volunteer job for the winter, a tutoring gig perhaps, and then I'd get to restart the garden in the spring. But the thought was useless, unless I wanted to switch to a public school, which would probably give my mom a stroke after everything she'd done to secure my spot at East Point. I tried to accept it, and just feel lucky for the time I'd been given.

"Darcy." I turned around to see Lucy and Damien standing behind me. Lucy held out a bouquet of dandelions tied together with a long piece of grass. "We made this for you," she said.

"Thank you, Lucy and Damien." I said, taking the bouquet from her. "This is beautiful. It's one of the nicest things anyone's ever given me." Lucy smiled and skipped away, perhaps in search of more dandelions. Damien followed her.

...

After we finished in the garden and returned the kids to school, I said goodbye to Mr. Brooks and thanked him for the opportunity to spend time with his students.

"It was my pleasure, Darcy," he said. "I know you might get busy with your cleaning job again soon, but you're welcome back as soon as we get started again."

"Thank you," I said, knowing it would be summer before I had any free time again.

Ms. Rose smiled at me. I had a feeling that she and Mr. Brooks might want to continue spending time together. After all, it was a Friday evening, soon to be Friday night. I let her know that Sean and I would take the bus home, as usual.

"Are you sure?" she asked. "Because I don't mind driving you home."

"Totally sure," I said. "Have a great weekend. I'll see you on Monday."

I caught up with Sean, who was standing just outside the door, looking at his phone.

"Hey," I said. "You heading for the bus stop?"

"I guess so. My mom's having this cocktail party at our house tonight. I think she wants me to make an appearance."

"That sounds exciting." I thought about it, and couldn't remember a time when my mom had had more than one friend over at a time. The thought of her having a cocktail party made me chuckle inwardly. The amount of small talk she'd be expected to make would probably give her a brain aneurysm, but I couldn't blame her for her introverted ways. It was something I'd probably inherited.

"Do you feel like coming? My mom is getting a caterer because she doesn't like to cook for a lot of people, so there's going to be a ton of food, and she told me this morning that I could invite a friend so I don't get bored."

"Ok, cool," I said, trying to sound casual, but inside my chest my heart was racing. Sean had several friends from school, yet I was the one he wanted to invite. And as much as I wanted to stay with him, I didn't know if I was ready to meet his parents, especially during an elegant party. "But what about my clothes?" My leggings were dirty from kneeling on the ground, and I'd also wiped my hands on my sweatshirt a couple of times. The only other outfit I'd had on me was my school uniform, which I always kept stuffed in my backpack during gardening. "Should I put my uniform back on? It's probably going to be wrinkly."

"If it includes a skirt then yes," said Sean, trying to hold back a sly grin.

"Oh, well..." It was probably the most forward thing Sean had ever said to me, and even though it flattered me, it still took me by surprise.

"I was joking, of course. You don't need to change. My parents are pretty down to earth. They know we were just working with kids in a garden."

"Ok then." I used my hands to brush the dirt off my leggings and sweatshirt. Sean put his arm around my shoulder as we started walking toward the park, pulling me in a little closer. "I guess I'll just have to see you in your skirt another time."

CHAPTER

FIFTEEN

We got off of the bus across the street from a high-end strip mall, showcasing Italian bistros, eclectic cafes, and high-end boutiques. On our side of the street was a row of red brick townhomes, each with a second-level balcony and street-level patio. I knew the nicest Hyde Park homes, the ones with the sprawling lawns and huge oak trees in the front yards, were off the main roads, more than a stone's throw away from the city bus stops.

"My house is a few blocks away," said Sean. We walked down Paxton for about a quarter of mile until we reached a side-street, where we made a right turn. Large, brick houses with massive porches and huge white pillars stood on each corner. The houses were older and less spread out than in Indian Hill, but the fact that we were in an affluent neighborhood was still obvious.

"This is it," said Sean, when we reached a large stucco house with a stone chimney

. It looked like it belonged in the English countryside, surrounded by flower gardens and rolling hills.

"Are we going to be greeted by a butler when we walk in?"

"No, but there is a cleaning lady who comes every Monday, and landscapers who come by every couple of weeks." He took his keys from his pants pocket and unlocked the front door. It opened up to a dimly lit entryway. On the left was a wooden staircase, and on the right, what looked like a formal sitting room, with velvet couches and antique lamps. I followed Sean down a hallway that led to the kitchen. "Mom, I'm home," he called out.

"Oh good, 'cause I could use a little help." Sean's mom was in the kitchen, standing in front of a large island, stocked with a variety of aluminum food trays. The kitchen was immaculate, like something out of an interior design magazine. It was at least three or four times the size of mine, lined with gorgeous white cabinets and dark gray countertops. And Sean's mom fit into the picture perfectly. She wore a cream sweater and a beige apron. Every one of her shoulder length hairs was in perfect place.

"Mom, this is Darcy. We just finished up with gardening."

"Oh, hello," she said. "It's wonderful to meet you." She walked around to the other side of the island and held out her hand.

"It's wonderful to meet you too, Doctor James," I said, shaking her hand.

"I'm so glad Sean finally brought you over."

"Mom," Sean snapped.

"Oh Sean. Don't get uptight," she said. "It's just that he's mentioned you a couple of times, Darcy, and I thought you sounded nice. Now where did I put those bamboo serving platters?" She turned around and began looking at the array of cabinets in front of her. "I'm serving Asian fusion tonight, so I thought my bamboo plates would be best."

"They're in the cabinet over there." Sean pointed at the wall adjacent to his mom. "The one above the microwave."

"Oh yes, thank you, dear. You know, I love my kitchen, but sometimes I think it's too big. I'm always forgetting where I put things."

"You just need to cook more often if you want to remember where everything is," said Sean.

She looked at him and rolled her eyes. "Maybe when I retire. Until then I think he can make his own meals," she said, giving me a wink.

"I agree. Sean should be cooking you dinner."

"Exactly. After all, I did wipe his hiney for three years." She found the bamboo serving plates and set them down on the island.

"Why are you both ganging up on me like that?" Sean sat down at a stool in front of the island. He lifted one of the aluminum lids to peek inside the tray. "I'm too busy with schoolwork to cook for everybody."

"Then I guess we'll all have to be content with frozen meals and takeout for the foreseeable future."

"This food smells amazing," I said.

"It's from Ginseng. Everything on their menu is delicious." Dr. James took a pair of tongs from a drawer and began transferring spring rolls from an aluminum tray to one of her bamboo plates. I got up to wash my hands so I could help arrange the food. "I sure hope I have enough food for everybody. Does this look ok for about twenty guests?"

"You have plenty of food, Mom," said Sean. "She always worries that she'll run out even though she gets enough for like three-hundred people."

"Well, you know me, always a worrier. Especially when it comes to food. I didn't grow up like you did, you know."

"Where did you grow up?" I asked. I went back to the counter and used a couple of plastic forks to transfer a separate tray of spring rolls.

"Cleveland, in the '70s. It was a little turbulent at times. My dad got laid off from his job at the factory when I was little, and after that it took a while for him to find another high-paying job. My mom tried to make ends meet by selling clothes she made to people in the neighborhood, but even when they were both working regular jobs, it was a struggle to pay all the bills and buy groceries for a family of five people. That was one reason I decided to become a doctor. I knew early on that I wanted a job where I would always be in demand. And of course, I'm a problem solver by nature. If I see somebody with a problem, I want to fix it, so making sick and injured people better is something I feel called to do."

"And you're good at it too," said Sean. "Not all doctors are as good at what they do."

"Thank you, Sean. I'm good at what I do because I care about the patients, not just the salary."

"What kind of medicine do you practice?" I asked.

"I do internal medicine. And Sean's dad is a cardiologist. He works at University Hospital."

"Oh," I said, automatically perking up. "My mom is an ER nurse at University Hospital."

"Is that right? I wonder if they might know each other."

"A lot of dad's patients get referred from the ER," said Sean.

"I'll tell you one thing; if your mother is an ER nurse and a mom, then I know she's a hard-working woman."

I nodded in agreement. "She is. And she's a single mom, too."

"Well then, we might as well give her a cape and a mask 'cause she's a super hero."

I couldn't help but chuckle at her comment. "Good one, Mom," said Sean, rolling his eyes.

"You know for a middle-aged mom, I have got some good material." She wiped her hands on her apron and looked behind her. "Oh, Lord," she said. "It's almost six o'clock. My guests will be here soon. I need to go change. Could you two finish setting-up the plates for me? I'll only be a few minutes."

"Mmhmm," said Sean, opening another tray. "A few minutes is code for about an hour."

"It's fine," I said, waving my hand. "We've got this under control, right Sean?"

"Yep, but there might be a small spring roll tax."

"Don't you eat all my food," called Dr. James as she shuffled down the hallway toward the steps.

"I'll protect it," I said.

"Thank you, dear."

I'd finished plating a tray of spring rolls and was moving on to the dumplings. "I like your mom," I said after a moment.

"I thought you two would hit it off."

...

Less than an hour later, everything was ready for the party guests. Sean and I had finished setting up the food, including all of the sauces, and put out the ceramic appetizer plates and napkins. Sean's dad had come home from work and after a quick wardrobe change (which included a red Hawaiian shirt and khaki pants) headed straight for the wet bar in an alcove off the kitchen to pour himself a drink. He was just as relaxed and affable as Sean's mom. "I'm the bartender for tonight," he said. "I've been informed that I'm not getting paid though. Should I put out a tip jar?"

Sean asked him if we could each have a drink, so he made us virgin margaritas. "I wouldn't mind letting you two try a little wine or something," he said, "but then Sean wouldn't be able to use my car to drive you home later. And your mom might kill me."

I laughed at the thought. Mom hated killing the mice that got into our house, but she'd sure as hell be pissed if I was brought home drunk by someone she didn't know.

Sean's mom came down in a comfortable but elegant looking turtleneck sweater dress just as her first guests arrived. Sean and I said our hellos and finished our drinks before slinking off to the basement.

"We've got a pool table," said Sean, as I followed him down the steps off the kitchen. "Do you want to play?"

"Sure. I kind of suck at it though."

"Me too. At least, I suck compared to my dad."

Sean arranged the balls in the triangle, then broke, scattering them around the table way more effectively than I could have. "So that drawing I did of you. I hope you don't think I'm being a creep or anything."

"No. I don't think that. It was a nice surprise, actually." I took a shot, aiming for a ball that seemed perfectly aligned with both the cue ball and the pocket, but still managed to miss.

"I'm glad you like it," he said. He walked around the pool table, assessing his opportunities. When he finally took a shot, he made it. "That was just luck."

"You liar. You don't suck at all."

He shrugged. "You just happen to be worse than me." He took another shot, but missed that time.

From upstairs came sounds of animated laughter. "They sure are having fun up there."

"Yeah, I think they're all starting to get tipsy. Another hour or two and they'll be straight-up drunk."

I took my shot and missed. "Well, I think it's great that your parents are having a good time."

Sean laughed. "Yeah, you're right. They deserve to let loose once in a while. I'm just glad you're here to make it less awkward for me."

"That's funny. I always thought I made things more awkward."

"Nice try, but no. I mean, I don't know what you're like in every situation, but gardening was definitely better once you joined."

"Really?" Sean made a shot. He circled the table looking for his next move. I plopped myself down into a nearby leather armchair.

"Yeah. I mean, the kids all loved you. It made things easier for me and Mr. Brooks. Plus, I kinda like hanging out with you. You're nice and you laugh at my lame jokes."

"You kinda like hanging out with me?"

"I think you know I more than kinda like hanging out with you. I'm just trying to play it cool."

My heart pounded in my chest. The time for subtlety was over. It was time to up my game, and show Sean how I really felt. "What if you stopped?" I asked.

"Stopped what?"

"Playing it cool."

He leaned his cue stick against the table and slowly approached me, sitting down in the chair next to me. A small round table separated us. I put my hand on the table, looking over at him. A few seconds later, he put his hand next to mine, letting our pinkies overlap. He started to lean closer, putting his whole hand on top of mine. My heart started beating even faster and my palms sweated. The rest of my body tingled, and I felt an emotion I couldn't even describe. Nervous yet happy, scared yet excited. For the first time in my life, I was about to be kissed by a boy who I liked and who actually liked me back. It was one of life's too good to be true moments.

"Sean!" His mom's voice boomed from the top of the stairs like thunder after a flash of lightning, making both of us jump.

"Jesus," he said. "How does she know?"

"Sean," she yelled again, "Molly's here. Come up and say hello!"

A look of surprise covered Sean's face, and I couldn't tell if Molly's arrival was good or bad. "Should we go upstairs?" I asked.

"Um, yeah. Molly's a friend of mine. I didn't know she was coming, but I guess it makes sense since our moms know each other. Anyway, I'll introduce you to her. You guys will probably like each other."

He stood up and headed for the stairs as I followed. Between seeing the look of trepidation on Sean's face and having our alone time interrupted, I couldn't help but worry about the arrival of his friend Molly. I told myself to get a grip and tried to curb my jealous instincts as we ascended the stairs. I knew that

Sean could like me and still be friends with other girls. It wasn't a big deal.

Until we got upstairs and I saw her. She had been sitting in the living room looking at her phone, but stood up when she saw us walk in. "Sean," she squealed. He leaned in to give her a hug, one that lasted several seconds (not that I was counting). "It's so good to see you. I've missed you these last few weeks," she said.

"I didn't know you were coming, but yeah, it's good to see you too."

"I know. It was a last-minute thing. But I thought it would be fun to surprise you, which is why I didn't text or anything."

Molly's gaze shifted from Sean to me. She gave me a slight smile. She was wearing jeans that fit her perfectly, ripped above the knees, with brown boots and a dark green bohemian blouse. I'd seen her before, first in Sean's sketchbook and then in one of his photos. She was even more beautiful in person.

"This is my friend, Darcy," said Sean after a moment of awkward silence, as if he'd been hoping we would do the introductions ourselves.

"Hi Darcy," she said with a polite wave.

"Hi," I said back.

"Darcy and I met at Taft. She started volunteering there last month," said Sean.

"We came here straight from the school garden," I said, "which is why I look like this."

"Oh, that's great! I actually volunteered there over the summer. And then I got Sean to join me in the fall, but I ended up being super busy with Model UN and I couldn't keep it up. It's so good that you got involved, so Sean wasn't left deserted the whole time."

I nodded eagerly, feeling a little like a bobble head, trying to mask my insecurity with enthusiasm. From hearing her explanation, I gathered that Sean hadn't joined Taft's Junior Gardener's program on his own, but at Molly's behest. "Cool," I said, looking at Sean. I caught his eye for a second, before he turned his gaze to the floor.

"Yeah," he said. "It was great when Darcy joined." He looked back up at me and smiled meekly. I forced a smile back, but couldn't help wonder why he hadn't mentioned that Molly, the girl whose angelic face he'd taken the time to draw in his sketchbook before meeting me, had been the real reason he started volunteering at Taft.

"Those kids are cute but they're a lot to handle," said Molly, tucking her red locks behind one ear. "So where do you go to school, Darcy?"

"East Point Prep." I tried to sound matter-of-fact, hoping not to have the conversation in which I explained my precarious financial situation that required hours of my janitorial services each week.

"Ooh, fancy," she said. "Do you know Natalie Suarez? I've met her at a couple of Model UN conferences. She's really sweet."

"Yes, she is. And smart," I said.

"Yes!" Her green eyes sparkled. I had to admit, Molly was affable, on top of being a young Jessica Chastain look-alike. If Sean had feelings for her, I couldn't blame him. In fact, it was difficult for me not to feel a little entranced by her.

"So, what about you? Do you go to school with Sean?"

Molly waived her hand. "Oh no. I don't have an artistic bone in my body. I go to Oak Mount."

"That's a great school, from what I hear." Oak Mount, the school I would have hoped to attend if Norwood hadn't been outside the city limits, was the best public high school in Cincinnati. All of its students pass a rigorous entrance exam, while many are placed on a wait list hundreds of names long. So not only was Molly gorgeous, she was intelligent, and already working toward a future in diplomacy.

"Yeah, I like it. But I do miss Sean. He and I went to the same elementary school, and our moms were on the PTO together. And we still have a lot of the same friends. Speaking of that. . ." She turned her attention to Sean, crossing her feet at the ankles and angling her body to face his. "Did Benny tell you I saw him at a Model UN conference last week?"

"Oh yeah, I think he mentioned that," said Sean, scratching his head.

"He told me that he's been dating Ethan. I had no idea!"

"That's right, for about the last month. They seem pretty happy together."

I listened on to the conversation between Sean and Molly about Benny and Ethan, which eventually shifted to Jimmy and Serena, another newly minted couple. After a few minutes of watching them, seeing their natural chemistry, the way Molly smiled and the way Sean nervously smirked and looked down at his feet, I began to get flashbacks to Paige's party, feeling painfully like the third wheel yet again. Tonight, I had thought it was finally my turn to play the romantic lead with the guy I liked, but as it turned out I was only the understudy, and the star actress had shown up to reclaim her role. This time, there was no one else for me to turn to, so it seemed my only option was to exit the stage entirely.

Abruptly, I turned around and grabbed my backpack, which I'd stowed on the bottom landing of the stairs before the party guests arrived. "Hey, Sean," I said, interrupting his conversation with Molly. "I just remembered that I've got an essay due on Monday, and if I don't start it tonight, there's no way I'll finish on time."

"You're leaving?" He turned to look at me, his brows furrowed. "But how are you getting home? I was going to drive you."

"It's fine. My mom actually just texted me. She's in the neighborhood running errands so she's going to pick me up. Thank your parents for me. See ya! And nice meeting you, Molly!"

I ran out the front door before Sean had a chance to question me further. Of course, I had made up the part about my mom texting me, but I knew she was off work, and I was pretty sure that she would be able to pick me up. I quickly ran in the dark toward the main road until I was no longer in sight of Sean's house, then took out my phone to call her.

"Of course, I'll come get you", she said when I explained my whereabouts to her. "Just walk to the shopping center and wait for me there."

What I hadn't made up was the part about my essay for Ms. Rose. I had planned to start it the next day, but why not get a head start? It would certainly beat a night of comparing myself to a gorgeous Model UN star. For the first time since starting high school, I was happy with who I was. As disappointed as I was in losing my chance with Sean and in the fact that my job as East Point cleaner was about to resume, my time at Taft had given me a glimmer of hope for the future. I no longer wanted to be Paige or Maya, or even Molly. I was following my own path, one that was meant just for me. Ms. Rose had helped illuminate it for me and now I needed to keep her light shining. There was no time for a pity party. In fact, I figured it was best to avoid parties altogether going forward.

I kept running until I got back to the main road. From there, I could see the lights from the restaurants and shops to the left. I waited for a break in traffic, then darted across the street. Up ahead I could see an outdoor table situated just outside a coffee shop. Once I reached it, I took a seat to wait for my mom. A pang of disappointment hit my stomach when I thought about what might have happened if Molly hadn't come to Sean's house. What now was never going to happen. Tears welled up in my eyes, but I wiped them away as Mom pulled up along the curb in front of me.

"I expected you to be out a little longer," she said after I'd gotten into the car. "Did something happen?"

"No. I was just ready to leave. And I think I'm finally ready to start that essay for Ms. Rose. I want to get the word magic flowing before I lose inspiration."

"Well, great. I can't wait to read it."

After we got home, I went straight for the kitchen, hoping to find a suitable snack to fill the void I was trying not to feel.

"You want some popcorn?" asked my mom.

"Yes, please. Especially if it's movie theater butter."

"It definitely is." My mom put the bag in the microwave and started the timer. "You know, Darcy, I've been thinking," she said. "You've been so happy the last month, since you stopped your after-school cleaning and started volunteering. I'd hate to see you lose that sense of belonging that it's given you. So, I have an idea. I know our house has gone up in value since I bought it. If I make a few updates, I bet I can get a really good price for it. If we sell, I can use that money to pay for your school, and you can keep volunteering and doing the things that you love."

"Sell our house?" I said, more loudly than I'd meant to. "Where would we live?"

"I've already talked to your grandparents about it, and they said we can move back in with them. In fact, they'd love it if we moved back in with them. And it wouldn't be for forever, just until I save enough money to make another down payment on a different house. And who knows, maybe you'll want to go out of state for college. I can wait and see where you end up and buy a house close to you. The nice thing about being a nurse is that I can find work anywhere."

Her suggestion left me completely flabbergasted. From my point of view alone, it sounded totally perfect. But I knew it would be selfish to agree. I couldn't let her sell the house just to get me out of cleaning, not after all the work she'd put into buying it for us. "Mom, it's wonderful that you would even consider doing that, but I can't let you start over, not after all the time and money you've invested in this house. If you want to sell, you should sell, but not so you can pay for my school. I don't mind going back to cleaning. I do want to continue with volunteering, but I'm sure I can find opportunities on the weekends and over the summer."

"Darcy, I'm your mom. It's my job to take care of you. And I know how hard you work, so now I want to help make you happy."

"I'm happy with things the way they are. Trust me, you don't need to change anything."

My mom let out a sigh. "You know, I do remember what it was like to be in high school, just a little bit. And I know that being the only kid who stays after school to clean probably makes things hard for you socially. I should have considered that more when I first signed you up for East Point. It's just,"—she looked up, putting her hands up in the air—"at the time it seemed like such a good opportunity."

"Mom, it's ok. Really. It was a good opportunity. It still is. You don't need to regret anything. I might not win the school popularity contest or anything, but I've got friends, and they don't care that I clean. And I don't care about it anymore either."

"Ok," said my mom. She walked around to where I was sitting and put her arm around me. "You know, you're way more mature than I was at sixteen. I'm proud of you."

"Thanks, Mom." I leaned my head on her shoulder, feeling the bones underneath the smooth layer of skin. She'd gotten skinnier over the last couple of years. Maybe she was working too much, and unable to make enough time to eat a decent meal. I made a mental note to cook her breakfast the next morning. After a moment she let go. "I guess I better let you get to work, huh?"

I nodded. "Yep, I suppose it's time." I stood up and carried my backpack into my bedroom. I took my phone from my front pocket to plug it into the charger and saw a text from Sean. *I'm sorry if I did something to upset you*, it said. *Did you make it home ok?*

Maybe I had been a bit dramatic by running out of the party like I had, but still, I didn't regret it. *I'm home now, about to start writing my essay*, I said in reply. I started to tell him that I would see him soon, but then realized I didn't know when or even if I would see Sean again. I deleted the last part and instead typed *Sorry for running out so quickly. Everything's cool*. Then I hit send and opened my laptop. Another party had left me feeling emotionally drained, but it was time to forget about that. It was time to focus on myself.

SIXTEEN

Over the last few weeks, I've struggled with the task of defining myself. Many of my peers and the staff members of East Point Prep know me as the school cleaner, the student who stays after school to sweep, mop, polish windows, and sanitize the desks for discounted tuition. In fact, this is what many of my friends suggested I write about, knowing it set me apart from everyone else in the school. And while I understood their points of view—after all, being the school cleaner has been a big part of my life for the last two years—it just didn't feel like the facet of myself that I wanted to define me. Although I know that I am lucky for this unique opportunity that allows me to attend East Point Prep, I've been eager to explore additional activities that let my personality and talents shine. While my position at East Point highlights my work ethic and responsibility, it doesn't exactly allow me to focus on what I think matters most, for example, combatting climate *change or fighting against hunger. This realization thus put me in a bit of an identity crisis.*

At East Point Prep, I have often felt a bit like Cinderella, scrubbing the floors in my rags while the princes and princesses dance around to their various extracurricular activities; soccer, football, Drama Club, Student Council, and so on. I have to admit, I longed to be one of them. I yearned to belong, to be a part of the 'we.' Eventually, this yearning evolved, and became less about wanting to be like everyone else to more about wanting to use my time in a way that would have a larger impact. That's when my fairy godmother, Ms. Rose, interceded.

Because of Ms. Rose's generosity, I have spent the last month volunteering for the Junior Gardeners Program at Taft Elementary School. For four weeks, I was able to suspend my cleaning duties and instead go to Taft Elementary after school every Monday, Wednesday and Friday, where, along with the teacher who founded the program and another high school volunteer, I led the students on a walk to their community garden space, where we spent nearly two hours tending to and harvesting the plants, and then enjoying the fruits of our labor.

Gardening with the children at Taft Elementary is about more than watering and harvesting the plants. It's about fostering an appreciation for nature, teaching a sense of community, and making sure the kids have nutrient-rich food to eat. In the garden, caring for one another is just as important as caring for the plants. The garden provides a calm that I and many of the elementary students need at the end of a stressful day of school. It taught me more about myself than any other experience I've had recently, including the fact that I love working with children and could potentially have a future in teaching. So, while the process of defining myself may not be complete, as I think most people tend to evolve over their lifetime, what I now know is that I'm more than the school cleaner. Although I will go back to my cleaning duties, I know that I will continue to make time to volunteer with children, ideally in a capacity that allows us to connect with nature and practice environmental sustainability. Maybe I will follow in Mr. Brooks' footsteps by teaching at an inner-city school where I too can start an urban gardening program, or perhaps I'll start a nonprofit that teaches gardening to kids all around the city. The possibilities are endless and my contributions to the Junior Gardening program are just the beginning.

Writing the essay came easily once I got it started. I spent the entire weekend working on it, writing, revising, and editing. I was happy with it, but more importantly I was proud of myself for getting to where I was. Finally, I felt at peace with myself. I was a little cleaned out, but I could make it until graduation.

"How did your essay turn out?" asked Paige when we sat down for lunch on Monday. "I know how worried you were about it."

"It turned out great. I finally got it all figured out. How about yours?"

"Ok, I think. I didn't start revising it until last night. I've just been so busy. I helped my mom with a fundraiser for The Breast

Cancer Research Center on Saturday. And then I had like fifty tests to study for, plus SAT and ACT prep." Paige sighed.

"And I'm sure you will crush all of those."

"I hope so, but I need a break. Do you want to hang out this weekend? We can just watch Netflix at my place or something. Maybe Saturday night?"

"Yeah," I said. "I would love that." I rummaged through my lunch tote, feeling underwhelmed with the meal I had quickly packed that morning, consisting of a blueberry Greek yogurt, some corn chips, and a turkey sandwich with a thin layer of mayo. I bit into a corn chip. "So, I have to go back to swabbing the deck today."

"Oh, yeah. I almost forgot about that. What a bummer. I wish you didn't have to."

I shrugged. "Yeah, but it could be worse, I guess. At least I still have my weekends and summer free."

"So, what about Sean? You guys hung out a lot the last month. Are you going to keep seeing him?"

"I don't know. Maybe, but I have a feeling not." My stomach sank at the realization. The optimist in me hoped that Sean might stay in touch, but the realist in me knew that he had lots of other friends, and that if we no longer shared a common activity, there probably wouldn't be enough of a reason for him to keep me in his circle. After all, I hadn't heard from him since

Friday night after leaving him alone with Molly. Who knows? Maybe the two of them had picked up where he and I left off.

After lunch, we walked to Ms. Rose's classroom. I took my essay out of my folder and eagerly waited to hand it in.

"Pssst, Darcy." I turned to my left to see Tristan leaning forward from his seat, which was kitty-corner to mine. "I just wanted to tell you that you look nice today, and every day, but especially today."

"Um, thanks," I said. I was wearing my hair down, for the first time in months, with a red scarf tied around my head. I'd thought I looked nice, but I wasn't expecting any special attention from Tristan.

Paige rolled her eyes. "You're going to have to try a lot harder than that for another chance with her, Tristan."

"Why don't you let her make her own decisions, Paige," said Tristan.

"She's right," I said quietly. In a way, it was exhilarating to be at the center of their squabble. A year earlier, I never would have guessed that either Tristan or Paige would want anything to do with me, and now here they were arguing over my interests.

"All right, I understand," he said, leaning back in his chair. "But it's ok, 'cause I like a challenge anyway." I held Tristan's gaze for a moment, my stomach fluttering despite my best efforts not to take him seriously.

"Hand up your papers, please," said Ms. Rose, waltzing into the classroom with a stack of ACT and SAT books in her arms. I took the bundle of essays being passed up to me and proudly placed mine on top. Finally, identity crisis over, at least for now.

"I am so excited to read these." Ms. Rose collected the essays from everyone sitting in the front row. "I'll try my hardest to have them back to you by Friday. Today, I thought we would spend some time talking about the essay section of the SAT and ACT."

Paige groaned and put her face down in her arms for a second before looking back up.

"You ready to soak in some more test prep knowledge?" I whispered.

"Like I have a choice," she said.

I laughed, but secretly, I felt like a kid being treated to an ice cream. I was probably the only student at East Point Prep who wasn't enrolled in a fancy test prep course or studying with a private tutor, and I needed all the help I could get. I spent the duration of the class period taking detailed notes and listing the dos and do nots with specific examples. It was one of the most enjoyable and useful lessons I'd been given in recent memory, filled with Ms. Rose's wonderful anecdotes, like the time she stayed up all night in college to write an essay that her professor had said was written beautifully, but still couldn't give a passing grade to because she hadn't actually answered the prompt. "The prompt was to compare two texts that had similar themes," she explained. "After quickly reading it, I thought we could pick any two texts that we'd read in the class, but he wanted us to choose texts from a particular unit of the class, and if I'd read the prompt closely enough, I wouldn't have wasted my time writing about *Wide Sargasso Sea*. Although I love *Wide Sargasso Sea*, so maybe it wasn't waste of time, but I did fail that essay. The only time I ever received an F on an essay, and it wasn't because it was written poorly, but because it didn't read the directions closely enough."

"That professor sounds like an asshole," interjected Tristan. A few people snickered, but the profanity didn't faze Ms. Rose.

"Well, some professors are," she said. "When you start college, you have to prepare yourself for that. Chances are, you're all going to deal with it at some point."

The bell rang, and I stayed seated for a while as everyone else rose from their seats to move on to their next period. When the classroom emptied out a bit, I approached Ms. Rose. "This is for you," I said, handing her a box with a personalized coffee mug I'd made for her online. It had a bouquet of flowers on it with the words 'Best Teacher Ever' and her name at the bottom. "I know it's not much, but I just wanted to let you know how much I appreciate what you did to help me."

"Darcy," she said, opening the box like it was something from Tiffany and Co. "I love this. Thank you so much."

"Thank you for giving me the chance to volunteer at Taft. It was a great experience."

"Well, Mr. Brooks really enjoyed having you there to help. I know you can't go back this spring, but they do have a summer program, so if you're free over the summer and want to..."

"I'd love to," I said.

"Great! Just send him an email at the end of the school year."

The next wave of students was entering the classroom. "Will do," I said. "See you tomorrow."

I walked to German feeling invigorated. I might have had to give up gardening, for now, but at least I still had Ms. Rose.

...

Paige found me at my locker after school. "Please don't let Tristan ooze his way back into your life. You and I both know he is not good boyfriend material."

"I don't think he's being all that serious, Paige. He probably just likes the attention."

"Well, good. I'm glad you see through his poor attempts at charming you."

"Doesn't mean I can't make out with him again though."

Paige gasped. "You wouldn't do that, would you?"

"I don't see why not," I lowered my voice to a whisper, so the wrong people wouldn't hear. "He is a good kisser."

"Darcy, what you need is a dependable boyfriend, not a playboy. And it can't be that hard to find someone else who can kiss. So, if Sean is out of the running, at least for now, then I need to work on finding you someone else. I know! Maybe Tom can set you up with somebody. A mature college guy is just what you need!"

I chuckled at Paige's eternal quest to make my life as perfect as hers. "Paige, I'm good. Really. Anyway, I have to go check in with the office for my cleaning assignment."

"Ok, I'll let you go, but I'm asking Tom to recruit one of his cute, single friends for you."

"Bye, Paige," I said as I headed for the office. I hoped that ignoring her last announcement would discourage the action she was threatening to carry out, but I never could tell with her. At least with all of her meddling, I knew that she cared about me.

I walked into the office, where Mrs. Hammerman was waiting with a welcoming smile on her face. "Hello, dear. It's so wonderful to see you in here again. I heard you got a little time off. How was it?"

"Really good. I got to hang out with elementary kids in a garden. It was perfect."

"Too bad it couldn't last, huh?" she said, handing me the clipboard.

"I'm hoping to go back over the summer. But for now, it's back to cleaning."

"You sure are a trooper, honey. Have a good afternoon."

"Thank you, Mrs. Hammerman."

I went to the supply closet to get the necessary items when I felt a vibration coming from my sweater pocket. *I'm in front of your school. Can you come outside?*

I re-read the message, wondering if it was a mistake. Was it meant for someone else? Perhaps, Molly? Why would Sean be standing outside of East Point Prep? I walked over to the vestibule in front of the main entrance, spray bottle and broom in hand, and looked outside. Sure enough, there stood Sean, standing halfway down the long row of concrete steps, wearing the olive-green hoodie that suited him so well.

I smoothed down my hair and took in a deep breath, hoping not to reveal how shaky my limbs were and how quickly my heart was beating. "What are you doing here?" I asked after I'd pushed open the doors. I set down my bottle and leaned my broom against the brick wall. My heart wanted me to leap down the steps toward him, but I did my best to take them one at a time.

"You left this at my house." Sean held out the marble patterned stainless steel water bottle that my grandparents had given to me for my birthday the year before. I'd always had it with me on gardening days, but hadn't even realized it was missing since leaving his house.

"Thank you. It must have fallen out of my backpack." I took the water bottle from his hand, lightly brushing my fingers against his. "Did you really come all the way here just to return my water bottle?"

Sean shrugged. "I thought you might need it, and I know these things aren't cheap to replace. Plus, I was hoping to see you in your school uniform."

My heart danced. "So, what do you think?" I twirled around to give him the full view.

"It's cute." Sean grinned and looked down at his feet. Of all the guys I knew, he was the only one who could turn ogling me in my skirt into a wholesome interaction.

"Thanks for bringing this. I wish I could hang out but I have to go back inside to clean."

"Oh yeah, there's one more thing." Sean ran down to the bottom of the steps and pulled out a bucket that had been hidden behind the bushes. It appeared to be filled with spray bottles, rags and some rubber gloves. I stared for a moment in confusion. Did he really think I wanted a bucket full of cleaning supplies?

"Is that for me? Because that's nice and all but the school provides all of the supplies I use."

"No. These are for me." Sean ran back up to where I stood on the steps. "I'm going to clean with you."

"You don't have to do that," I said, uncertain as to whether or not he meant it seriously.

"I know, but I want to."

"Really?"

"Yeah, you know, to keep you company."

"Well, ok, if you want. I'll take the company." I ran up to the door and poked my head inside, my knees shaking in excitement and nervousness. Sean coming to my school with the intention to help me clean was another too good to be true moment. Suddenly, I was even more glad that I'd taken the time to look nice that morning. I just hoped we wouldn't get busted.

A lone freshman was sitting on the bench in the vestibule, probably waiting for her ride. "I think we're ok. Follow me and act natural," I said, grabbing my spray bottle and broom.

"Do you think I'll get kicked out?" he asked.

"I don't know. You're probably the first student from a different school who's wanted to sneak in to help sanitize."

"It does sound ridiculous when you put it like that." Laughter burst out from my mouth, and I put my hand over it to keep it contained. Only Sean could rebel while simultaneously doing something immensely useful that would likely make every adult proud.

As we walked into the school, I looked side-to-side, ensuring Mrs. Masterson wasn't in the hallway. "We have to be covert," I said. Supplies already in hand, we tiptoed down the hallway, then quickly crept through the door leading to the stairwell and went to the second floor. We went from room to room, turning the corners with our backs to the wall, like people out of a cheesy spy movie, avoiding rooms that were still occupied by teachers. At one point we skulked our way into a room that looked empty from the hallway, pulling out our best secret agent moves, using the spray bottles as props, saying, "all clear," as we entered, only to see Mr. Braun, the Spanish teacher, sitting in a desk in the back of the classroom with two of his students, apparently reviewing test grades. They all stopped what they were doing and looked at us with furrowed brows as we slowly backed our way out into the hallway without saying a word.

We ran to the end of the corridor before bursting out into laughter. "Those were some good moves back there. I think you're a natural born spy," said Sean.

"Sean? What are you doing here?" We turned to see Ms. Rose standing in front of us, a large stack of essays in her arms.

"I'm sorry, Ms. Rose. Please don't kick me out," he said, as we both tried to regain our composure.

"He's just helping me clean. It was totally my idea."

"It's ok. I'm not kicking you out," she said after looking around. "Although, if you want to keep this up, you'll probably want to keep a lower profile."

"Ironically, we did get a little carried away with our spy act. But I swear, it's just for today," I said.

"Ok then, you two," she said with a smirk. "Just try not to have too much fun." She started to walk through the door that led to the stairwell, then leaned in toward me. "He's a keeper, Darcy," she said into my ear. It was quiet, but not exactly a whisper.

I smiled and looked at Sean, who was doing his best to nonchalantly look around, as if he hadn't heard Ms. Rose's remark. "So, what's next?" he asked.

"I guess we'll head up to the third floor and then come back here to hit the rooms that we missed on the way out."

"All right then, you lead the way."

I grabbed the broom and tiptoed my way into the stairwell, like Elmer Fudd from the old-timey Looney Tunes cartoons, with Sean laughing and walking behind me. "So much for being covert," he said.

We finished wiping down the desks, sweeping the floors and emptying the trash cans in the rest of the rooms on my list, all the while listening to a playlist on Sean's phone. He gave me one of his wireless ear buds so I could hear his favorite songs by A Tribe Called Quest. After we finished, we returned the broom and spray bottles to the supply closet and went outside through the front door. We walked down the steps, and without even thinking I plopped down on one of the benches in front of the school to give my feet a rest.

"That was really fun," I said. Sean put down his bucket and sat down beside me. "You know, you're the only friend who's ever helped me, and you don't even go to this school."

Sean shrugged. "I knew you were kind of bummed about having to start cleaning again, so I just thought you could use some support."

Sean had always proven himself a good friend by helping me in the garden and taking me out to dinner, but until then, I hadn't realized how much I'd be able to depend on him. I had thought our friendship had formed and been held together by convenience, and that having the convenience removed would dissolve whatever bond we'd created. But he proved me wrong. He'd shown up when I least expected it when he literally could have gone anywhere else. Ms. Rose's words echoed in my mind. 'He's a keeper'. It was true, but did he want to be kept?

"I'm sorry about the way I left your house on Friday. Seeing you and Molly together made me a little insecure," I said, finally addressing the elephant in the room.

"I'm sorry you felt that way. I shouldn't have let that happen."

227

"It's ok. You can talk to anyone you want. I mean, it's not like I'm..." I couldn't say the words *your girlfriend*. I couldn't let him think I was suggesting it, even though I wanted to.

"Darcy." Sean moved his body sideways on the bench, facing me more directly. "Molly's a good friend of mine. I've known her since we were kids and we hang out with a lot of the same people, but I don't like her like that." I turned toward him. He took my hand in his and I looked up, meeting his eyes. "I mean, I did at one time, and I guess that's the main reason I joined Junior Gardeners. But I stayed because I really liked it. I liked the kids, and Mr. Brooks, and being outside in the garden. And then you showed up and it was even better. I like you, Darcy."

I repeated his words in my head, letting them linger. It was a simple phrase. *I like you*. But it was the first time I'd heard them from a guy that I liked, which made them monumental. I looked at his face, less than a foot away from mine, and without another thought leaned in and put my mouth against his. A second later he was kissing me back, putting his hands around my waist to pull me in closer.

After a moment there were voices coming from the parking lot. I looked over to see Tristan, Matt, and a few other football players getting into their cars. Tristan stared in our direction, a baffled grimace plastered onto his face. "Who's that guy?" asked Sean.

"Tristan. He's in my English class."

"He doesn't look very happy."

"I think he's just confused."

"He thinks I'm invading his territory."

"His territory does not include me."

Sean laughed and put his arm around me. "Indeed. You are a sovereign state."

We watched as Tristan and the others got into their cars, hooting and hollering about a kegger that someone from the team was supposedly planning for the weekend.

"You know, I'm glad we don't have sports at my school," said Sean.

"You don't have any sports?"

"Nope. We're far too sophisticated for those locker room antics. Actually, it's probably because we don't have enough money."

"I wish I had some kind of artistic talent so I could switch to your school," I said.

"I bet you do. You could try chorus, or drama maybe."

I chuckled at the thought of attempting to sing in front of a panel of judges, shattering glass, but not in the glass ceiling sort of way. "You've never heard me sing. And I don't think I can act either. Whenever I'm in front of an audience my face turns red and my voice quivers."

Tristan pulled his car around the front of the school. "Hey, Darcy," he shouted as he drove by.

"Then again, maybe I could give it a go," I said.

"Is this the guy that you told me about before? The one who let you get away?"

I nodded. "How'd you guess?"

"I just had a feeling about it. And I was right about him being an idiot. Just let me know if he gives you any trouble at school, ok?"

"Ok. I will." I knew I didn't need Sean, or any to protect me. but I still liked knowing that he had my back.

My phone buzzed in my pocket. Mom had messaged me, letting me know that she was on her way home and could pick me up if I needed a ride. "Do you want a ride? My mom can bring you home."

Sean grinned a toothy smile at me. "I have a surprise for you," he said.

"What? A surprise? Just you being here was a surprise!"

"Come with me. Your chariot awaits." He stood up and held out his hand. I grabbed my backpack and walked with him into the parking lot, which was almost empty by then. A few rows back was a black Toyota Corolla. Sean took a key fob from his pocket to unlock it, making it beep twice.

I gasped, covering my mouth with my hands. "This is yours?"

"Yep, as of yesterday afternoon. It's an early birthday present." Sean walked around to the passenger side and opened the door.

"It's beautiful. And it's a hybrid," I said. I quickly texted Mom to let her know I was getting a ride and would see her at home soon. A ride from my boyfriend. Although, I wasn't really sure if the boyfriend title was official yet.

Sean knew the way from my school to my house without asking for directions or using his phone, and I wondered if he had already looked up the route or if he was a naturally good navigator. As he drove, he filled me in on the assignments he had to do for homework and volunteer opportunities he was considering for the winter, including something at Taft Elementary called Reading Buddies. When he got to my house, he pulled into the driveway and put the car in park. I lingered for a moment, just looking at him, soaking up the happiness. I didn't want to leave him yet, but we could only sit in in his car in my driveway so long.

"Thank you for the ride," I said.

"It was my pleasure," he said. He took my hand in his and brought it up to his lips.

"I should probably go into my house now."

"Then I guess I should probably let you go."

We both said goodbye as I got out of the car, and I realized as I walked into my house that I didn't know what to do next. It was all new to me, the concept of having a boy who I liked like me back. I didn't know what any of it meant beyond that day. I didn't know hoe often we would talk, or how often we would see each other. I didn't know at what point I would need to introduce him to Mom. But maybe I was wasting my brain energy on something that wouldn't even last. I told myself to stop worrying and to just let myself be happy for once. I took a deep breath and went inside my house. One thing was certain: I needed to talk to Paige.

SEVENTEEN

P aige answered her phone after the second ring. "Hey, Darcy. What's up?"

"Me and Sean kissed!"

"What? When?"

I told her the story, starting with how Sean had shown up to help me clean and every detail that happened afterwards. "Darcy, this is amazing! I knew you would find a boyfriend soon!"

I sighed. "I don't know if I can officially call him that. That wasn't something we discussed."

"Well, you need to discuss it, ASAP! No more kissing until he commits."

"But what if pressing him on it scares him away? I don't want to come across as needy. Not everyone needs labels, right?"

"Look, Darcy, if he wants to keep spending time with you, then a simple label isn't a lot to ask. It's not like it's marriage or anything. It's just to clear up any confusion and make it less complicated."

I told her that I would wait a couple of weeks, and that if there was still any uncertainty about it, I'd inquire about it then. But luckily, I didn't have to. The very next day, Sean came to pick me up after I finished cleaning.

"I could get used to this," I said as he opened the car door for me.

"I don't have anything else going on after school right now. The least I can do is give my girlfriend a ride."

A smile spread across my face like a pat of butter on a warm piece of bread. I couldn't have contained it if I'd wanted to. "Are you ok with me calling you that?" he asked.

I nodded. "Yes, I am."

He drove me home with one hand on the steering wheel and the other on top of mine. Mom's car was already in the driveway, so I knew she was home. "Do you want to come inside?" I asked him.

"Do you think your mom will like me?" he asked.

"I don't see how she couldn't."

"Ok, then. Let's do it."

Mom was pulling items out of the refrigerator when we walked in. She nearly dropped a package of ground turkey when she saw us, but her eyes lit up like fireworks after I introduced her to Sean. "Will you stay for dinner? I'm making tacos."

"Taco Tuesday! Yes, please!" said Sean.

He and I set the table while my mom cooked. I grabbed us each a Coke from the fridge and poured my mom a glass of wine from an open bottle. She asked him questions about his school and his family without sounding like a manager giving a job interview. I gushed about his drawing talent, and he promised to bring his sketchbook into the house the next time he came over. When he was ready to leave, my mom gave him a hug, insisting that she was a hugger (although I knew for a fact she wasn't), and I walked outside with him to his car. He put his hands on the side of my face and gave me a gentle kiss before getting into his car and driving away. Everything about the evening was perfect, like in the beginning of a Lifetime movie before the protagonist realizes that her boyfriend is a serial killer, only I knew Sean wasn't secretly a serial killer. Everything really was as wonderful as it appeared.

And things continued to go that way. The next week, Sean started to volunteer for the Reading Buddies program, so I didn't see him after school as often, but we still talked on the phone most nights and saw each other every weekend. At first, we went on dates by ourselves, to the Indian restaurant or movie theater Uptown, but after a couple of weeks, Sean took me to Tyler's house so I could meet some of his friends.

"Thanks for agreeing to go with me," said Sean after he picked up. "Tyler wouldn't stop asking about when he was going to meet you."

"Really? He's that eager to meet little old me?"

"Of course he is. I talk about you all the time."

I blushed. "I talk about you all the time too."

Sean's smile was enough to make me melt into my chair. He could've not taken me anywhere. He could've just driven me around all night, holding my hand, and I would've been happy. But when he pulled up to Tyler's house, Sean was beaming, and I knew he was excited to introduce me to everyone. "You ready to go in?" he asked. I nodded and hopped out of the car.

Tyler and a few other people were sitting inside the open garage. Tyler was tall, like Sean, but a bit lankier. He wore a pair of ripped jeans and a plaid shirt with the sleeves rolled up, which I eventually realized was his signature look. "Sean, it's about time you got here, man," he shouted as we approached. "And you must be Darcy."

"I am. It's nice to meet you."

Tyler clapped Sean on the back and pulled me in for a hug, as if he'd known me for years. He introduced me to Tess, Zane and Hoover. "Thank God I'm not the only girl anymore," said Tess.

Tyler made a big show about finding an extra folding chair and putting it next to Tess so that the two of us could sit next to each other. His demeanor was the opposite of Sean's, boisterous and a bit arrogant. It would have been impossible to be in the same house as him and not know he was there, even if it were a sprawling mansion. But his friendliness made up for the volume, and I could see how his intensity was balanced out by Sean's calmness.

Tess and I sat quietly for what felt like several minutes while the guys talked music. Zane, Tess's boyfriend, was studying music production at the Academy for the Arts, and was going into detail about how the album playing was produced while Sean and Tyler asked questions and made comparisons to different albums. Tess looked at me and rolled her eyes. I laughed and shrugged. "Do you know what they're even talking about?" I asked.

"I never do." She cleared her throat, but when that failed to get their attention, she stuck her fingers in her mouth and made a loud whistle. The guys stopped talking and turned their heads to look at us. "Hello. We're bored over here. Can we play a game or something?" asked Tess.

Tyler clapped his hands aggressively. "Wonderful idea, Tess!" He rearranged the chairs to form a circle and grabbed a large glass jug from the fridge behind him. "Let's play I Never with my dad's homebrewed kombucha. It's only *slightly* alcoholic, so you'll all be able to drive home tonight."

Sean sat next to me. "You ready for this?" he asked.

"I guess so. Should I be nervous?"

"Nah. I'm not going to judge you for anything." He smiled and squeezed my knee.

Tyler passed around some cups and started filling them up with the kombucha. "Buckle up, Darcy. You and Sean are about to learn more about each other than you might want to." He winked at me as he filled my cup.

The *I Nevers* started out somewhat tame. I never spent an entire day watching Netflix or playing video games. I never snuck into a movie at a theater. I never wrote the important dates on the palm of my hand before a history quiz. I never lied to my mom about where I was or who I was with. I drank for all but the movie theater. Sean drank for all of them.

It was Hoover's turn to state an *I Never*. "I'm going to keep this one simple. I've never had sex."

Tess giggled as she raised her cup to her mouth. Tyler, Zane and Hoover all chuckled as they drank. I looked at Sean, more than half-expecting him to be drinking like everyone else. But like me, he sat there with his cup down at his lap. Our eyes met, and I smiled at him, hoping he couldn't tell how hot my cheeks were burning with the realization that all of his closest friends knew we hadn't reached that milestone yet.

Tyler belched. "I had to take an extra big gulp for that one. And trust me, Darcy, the reason Sean didn't drink isn't because he hasn't had the opportunity. I can tell you that for certain."

I raised an eyebrow at him.

"He just has higher standards than I do."

Tess and Zane laughed. "And I'm sure the same goes for Darcy," said Tess. "But, now that you two have each other." She nudged me with her elbow, and my face burned even hotter. My virginity wasn't something I wanted so prominently on display.

"Maybe next time we'll all be able to drink to that one." Zane slapped Sean on the back of his shoulder and gave him a not so coy wink.

"Will you guys cut it out?" said Sean. "Darcy and I don't need you sticking your noses in our business."

I smiled at him as he put his arm around my shoulders. I mouthed the words *thank you*, and he kissed my cheek in response. The conversation moved on as Tess took her turn with the next *I Never*, but I couldn't stop thinking about me and Sean and whether or not we would ever take our relationship to that level. It was something I wanted, but not for the sake of a drinking game.

We played the game until the jug of kombucha was empty. Tyler, Tess and Zane had needed refills, while I still had plenty left from my first pour. I slowly sipped it while the guys talked and Tess painted my nails with a bottle of blue nail polish she'd had in her purse. At eleven o'clock, Tyler's parents returned from their night out, which everyone took as a signal to leave.

"So, that was interesting," said Sean while driving me back home.

"Your friends must think I'm pretty boring. They all drank way more than me."

"You're not boring. You just make good choices."

"Like saving myself for you. That was a good choice." I smiled and looked down at my lap, surprised by the boldness of my statement. It was the first time I'd brought it up with him, but now that it had been discussed by all of his best friends, it seemed silly to still be shy about it.

"Really? You mean, you want to?" Sean looked at me, his eyes alert and inviting.

"Well, not right now, but yes, eventually."

"Cool. I like the sound of that," said Sean, nodding emphatically. "I mean, no pressure, but I'm ready when you are."

Sean took his right hand off the steering wheel and placed it on my lap. I put my left hand on his, letting his fingers graze my thigh. A part of me didn't want to wait, but I knew I wasn't ready yet, and if he could be patient, so could I.

CHAPTER

EIGHTEEN

" I broke up with Tom over the weekend," said Paige, removing the peel of a mandarin orange on her lunch tray.

I nearly spit out the sip of coconut, mango seltzer water I'd just taken. "Really? Why? What happened? Everything seemed fine between you two on our double date."

Paige cocked an eyebrow at me. "You mean how you, me and Sean played skee-ball while Tom sat at our table like he was too good for a single arcade game. He was acting like a total stuffed-shirt. It was embarrassing."

"I didn't realize it bothered you. Is that really the reason you dumped him, or is there more to it?"

"I guess once the honeymoon phase of our relationship ended, it didn't feel like there was much there."

"But you only saw each other every couple of weeks. How did the honeymoon phase end so quickly?"

Paige shrugged. "I realized a few weeks ago that I might not like him as much as I thought I did at first. I was attracted to him, but that's not enough to keep a relationship going, especially when he kept making it so complicated. One week he was hot and the next he was cold. I finally got to a point where I couldn't take the drama anymore. I want to be with someone more easy-going, like Sean."

"Like Sean?"

"Darcy, I'm not going to steal your boyfriend. Even if I wanted to, it wouldn't work. He only has eyes for you. I just wish I could find someone *like* him. Someone who doesn't make things hard."

"Paige, I'm floored. I never expected to be the one in the model relationship. I mean, I'm sorry. Are you going to be ok?"

She sighed. "I think so. It's disappointing, but I know what I want, and I don't want to waste any time on something I know isn't that, especially when it's not even all that fun."

"So, you feel good about it?"

She nodded. "Yep. No regrets. He didn't even try to change my mind, so it appears I made the right decision."

"Well, Paige, cheers," I said, holding up my can of seltzer water, clinking it with her can of Diet Coke. "To your newfound independence. I think this will be a good change for you. About how many days do you think it will take you to find a new boyfriend?"

"Shut up," she said with a smirk.

"Oh, I know. You probably need me to help you find one. Here, let me check Instagram and see who I can find for you." I began to open up the app on my phone, scrolling through my friends and saying, "Hmmm," and, "Maybe," every few seconds.

"Shut up," she said again, throwing a crouton from her salad across the table at me.

"Ok, ok." I said, laughing, and tucked my phone back into my backpack. "I only have like ten mutuals on there anyway."

"Hey guys, can I sit with you?"

I turned around to see Maya standing behind me with her tray of cafeteria food. "Um, yeah, sure," I said.

Paige nodded with a tight-lipped smile. "Yeah. The more the merrier," she said.

Maya pulled out a chair and sat directly between me and Paige. She smiled uncomfortably as she mixed the dressing into her salad. The three of us sat quietly, apparently all waiting for someone to break the silence. "I'm sorry if I interrupted something," said Maya.

"You didn't interrupt anything," I said. I looked at Paige, wondering if her expression would contradict my statement, but she didn't look annoyed in the slightest.

"I broke up with my boyfriend. I was just telling Darcy about it. So, that's the tea."

"Oh, I'm sorry to hear that."

"It's ok. I'm not really that upset at the moment. But the reality of not having a boyfriend might hit me eventually, and then I'll probably be in shambles."

"You'll be great, Paige," I said, patting the back of her hand. "Just think of all the fun you can have now, and all the anxiety that you've saved yourself from." I turned to Maya, trying to think of some sort of transition. "How are you and Matt?" I asked nervously, hoping Paige's feelings for Matt hadn't changed now that she was single.

"We're good." I noticed Maya looking over at him. He and Tristan and a couple of other guys from the football team were sitting a few tables over. Matt seemed unaware of our gaze on them. Tristan, on the other hand, was looking directly at us, wearing a smug smirk. "I've just been feeling like maybe we spend too much time together, so I was thinking it might be nice if I could join you two for lunch sometimes. Would that be ok?"

"You mean you don't enjoy eating your lunch surrounded by a bunch of numskulls?" asked Paige. "That doesn't include Matt, by the way. He's just guilty by association."

Maya laughed, biting into a slice of pizza. "I know Tristan can be a jerk, but that's mostly because he thinks it impresses everyone. One-on-one, he's not so bad. He's actually kind of a softie."

He had been a softie with me, at one time. "Well, yeah. I think it's cool if you want to eat lunch with us," I said.

Paige was looking down at her tray, chewing a bite of salad. "Mmmhmm," she said, without opening her mouth.

"Cool." Maya smiled and relaxed her shoulders. "I've missed having girl time."

"Me too," I said. And I had missed having girl time with Maya, but so much had changed since the start of the school year. I'd made an entire new best friend, and I didn't know how easy it would be to have two. I worried that the two of them wouldn't get along. Or that they might become best friends with each other and leave me on the outskirts. I even wondered for a split second if Maya's claim of wanting more 'girl time' was really just a plot to sabotage my friendship with Paige. Afterall, she had stolen my crush.

But that was going too far, and I knew it. Maya had apologized for what happened with Matt, and I believed her to be sincere. I had forgiven her, and now it was time to make an effort to be her friend again. I had to trust her, and trust that my friendship with Paige was strong enough to adjust to some changes.

Over the next few minutes, we continued chatting about Paige and Tom's breakup, the ups and downs of Maya's relationship with Matt, and my own relationship with Sean. "I hope I can meet him soon," said Maya.

"They're adorable together," said Paige.

Thinking about Sean made me smile. I was proud to be his girlfriend, not because I'd been desperately hoping for a boyfriend since freshman year, but because I really liked him, maybe even loved him. Yes, I loved him, although I hadn't said it aloud to anyone yet. I loved him for being considerate, for consistently thinking of my needs before his own wants. I loved him for being artistic and intellectual. I loved him for being a good role model, for choosing to volunteer with underprivileged kids, not because he needed to in order to impress colleges, but because he wanted to. The only thing that was missing right now was being able to do that with him. I knew the chance would come along in the summer, but in dreary December, summer seemed like such a long way away.

By the time lunch ended, my anxieties about Maya had faded. Even Paige, who seemed a little cold and tense at first, had loosened up and appeared to enjoy the additional company. "Thanks, Paige," I said to her as we walked to English class together.

"Thanks for what?" she asked.

"For being so cool with Maya. I was worried you might not get along with her."

"Any bad feelings I had toward Maya were out of support for you. But if you're over it, then I guess I should be too. And you know, once I started giving her a chance, I actually liked her."

I put my arm around Paige, giving her a side hug as we approached Ms. Rose's classroom. It seemed almost outlandish to think that just a few months earlier I had offered to clean her house so I could go to her party. Since then, we'd both evolved so much. It was like we were two pieces of a puzzle that had been stuck in the wrong spaces, but now we were positioned in the right spot and everything fit together perfectly. I guess that's what life is, a jigsaw puzzle that just keeps growing and changing as some pieces fall away and others fit into place. And, given the circumstances, the puzzle of my life was feeling almost as complete as it could. There were a few gaps here and there, but the edges were coming together, and it was looking wonderful.

CHAPTER

NINETEEN

It was winter break, and Christmas was less than a week away. I had started to pick up babysitting jobs a couple of weeks earlier so that I could save up some money to buy gifts. I had my mom advertise my services on the online neighborhood forum she's on, letting other members know that I was available on Friday and Saturday nights, and she started receiving requests almost immediately.

One of the families had a toddler. She was really cute, but cried for her mom for the first forty-five minutes. I finally calmed her down after finding the remote for the TV and putting on Daniel Tiger. I gave her some crackers and milk from a sippy cup, and after the show was over, helped her change into a Disney Princess nightgown. She proudly named all of the princesses for me. "'Dis one's Jasmine, 'dis one's Cinderewa, 'dis one's sweeping beauty and 'dis one's Tiana."

"They're beautiful, just like you," I said, helping her into her little bed with a mesh rail to keep her from rolling out. I left her lamp on until she fell asleep, as instructed by her mom. A few minutes later she was crying because she couldn't find her favorite stuffed dog. I helped her find it under the bunched-up blanket, then covered her back up.

"Will you stay with me?" she asked.

"Sure." I took a seat in the glider in the corner of her room and hummed lullabies to help her fall asleep. When I could tell she was fully asleep, I turned off her lamp and crept back downstairs. I was exhausted after just a couple of hours, and couldn't imagine doing it every single night. Although, I suppose people with their own kids get used to it, like I'd gotten used to cleaning after school.

The extra work kept me busy, and made it harder to spend time with Sean, but all in all I'd made over three hundred dollars, which was enough to buy something for everyone on my relatively short list. The gift I was most excited to give was Sean's.

On the first day of break, Paige drove me to an art supply store near the University, and I asked the young, heavily tattooed woman who worked there to show me the best set of pencils I could buy for a serious artist. She walked down one of the aisles and came back with a small tin box with a French name on the label. "These are the best pencils we sell," she said. "They're not cheap, but they're worth it. They'll make a great gift."

Paige balked at the price. "Are you sure you want to spend a hundred dollars on a box of pencils?"

I thought for a moment, then nodded. "Yep, I do. Sean deserves it."

She sighed. "He better get you something really good."

"I don't care if he does or not." I took my wallet from my bag and counted out enough cash to make the purchase. "I'm just happy to give something nice to him."

"Ok. It's your money," she said with the tone of a concerned parent.

I laughed and gave her a pat on the shoulder. "I know. I know. It will all be ok." The tattooed woman took my money and gave me the pencil box in a little paper bag with handles.

"I wish I had a boyfriend to buy a gift for. Maybe I should have waited until after the holidays to break up with Tom."

"Just take the money you would have spent on him and buy something nice for yourself. Then you'll probably feel better."

"That's good advice. Do you want to go to the mall?"

"Sure. I still have a few more gifts to buy." We left the store and stepped out onto the sidewalk. It was a sunny day, warm enough for me not to need the fleece jacket I was wearing.

"Should we see if Maya wants to meet us?" Paige unlocked her car, which was parked just outside of the shop.

I hadn't expected Paige to want to include Maya, but I was glad that she did. It was official. The three of us were now a squad, and it had only taken a couple of weeks. "Good idea. I'll call her."

...

Paige dropped me off at my house later that evening, around dinnertime. Outside it was dark, but my street was well-lit with multi-colored strands of lights on many of the houses and trees lining the streets. Mom had wrapped some gold ones around the two little juniper trees on either side of the walkway leading to the front door. I walked in, carrying the bag with Sean's pencils and two other bags from the mall. I'd spent the day with my two best friends who were now also friends with each other, and I'd completed my Christmas shopping on top of that. My life was the least complicated it had been since I was a kid. I'd gone over some major bumps to get there, but they had been worth it.

When I went inside, Mom was sitting on the couch in the living room, biting her bottom lip, something she only did when she was worried. She stood up almost immediately and helped me put my bags on the floor. "I'm glad you're finally home," she said, her voice sounding a bit shaky.

"Is everything ok?" I asked. My first thought was that something had happened to one of my grandparents, but I knew she would have called if that had been the case.

"Yeah, everything's fine. Do you want to sit for a minute?"

We both sat down, her on the couch and me in the armchair next to it. I looked at her, waiting to hear what she had to say, my heart beating faster with every second that passed. I didn't know what she wanted to talk about, but I figured it had to do with the house. Maybe she'd decided to sell it once and for all.

She took a deep breath. "I know that you know about the circumstances surrounding your father, my relationship with him, and why he hasn't been in our lives. You've always been so understanding of it all. I don't know what it's like to grow up without a father, without even knowing who my father is. And yet you've done that, without ever complaining or showing any sign of resentment. I want to thank you for that, and let you know that I'm sorry you didn't get to have a dad like I did."

My stomach twisted at the mention of my father. It wasn't like my mom to bring him up out of nowhere. "It's ok. I mean, I had you, and Grandma and Grandpa. I guess I've been curious at times, but I understand why you made your choice to stop seeing him."

"I just wish you had gotten to know him," she said.

"What do you mean?" I asked, trying to hold back tears. "Is he dead?"

"Oh no," said my mom. Her ponytail, which was usually pulled back tight, was now loose, a few free stands hanging down around her face. "Not at all. I just meant that I wish you had gotten to know him when you were younger. But actually, I've been in contact with him recently. He and his wife just got a divorce, for reasons that have nothing to do with either of us, according to him anyway, and I guess he feels like he no longer has anything to hide. And now that you're older and can better understand why things happened the way they did, I don't really think I need to shelter you from the situation as much. So, he was wondering, would you like to meet him?"

"Meet him? Like in person? Face to face?"

My mom leaned forward, putting her hand on my knee. "Well yes, if you want to. He's very interested in meeting you, if you're willing to do it."

Meet my dad. See him in person. Talk to him. Try to get to know him. Try to help him get to know me, after sixteen years of living life without him. As overwhelming as it might seem, I knew without hesitation that I wanted to do it. "Yes," I said. "I am."

...

The next day I walked into the café where my dad had suggested meeting him for lunch, my legs shaky and my heart pounding. I almost turned and ran out the door, but Mom had probably already driven off. She'd already told me when I got out of the car that she was going to run an errand and come back in an hour, which meant I was stuck. I swallowed hard and took in a deep breath.

I looked around, having no idea if I would recognize him. A man in a corner table started to stand, smiling and waving at me nervously. I walked toward him, knowing I recognized his face, his slicked back wavy hair and wired-rim glasses. Where had I seen him?

"Look at you. So grown up, and beautiful, just like your mother," he said when I reached the table. "I knew it was you."

"Have we met before?" I asked, sitting down in the chair across from his.

"We didn't meet exactly, but I walked by you a few months ago. It was downtown, near Washington Park. You were standing outside a diner with a boy about your age. When I saw you, it felt like getting hit by a truck. You look so much like your mother. I just knew it was you. I wanted to stop and ask you your name, you know, verify my intuition. But I didn't want to catch you off-guard like that, without knowing whether or not you wanted anything to do with me." He paused for a moment, taking a slurp from his coffee mug. After setting the mug down he continued. "So, I just kept walking, but I kept thinking about it, week after week, until I finally decided to get in touch with your mom. And I'm very grateful you know, that you agreed to meet me. I'm sorry it's taken so long. Sometimes I wish things had been different, but I guess you know the circumstances, and why it was so complicated."

I took it all in, then began to laugh. "If only I'd known," I said. I told him about Sean's interpretation of the event, and his comment about him being old enough to be our dad. "But I never would have guessed that you actually were. I didn't think we would ever randomly cross paths."

"I always wondered," said Greg, wagging his pointer finger in the air ever so slightly. "I always wondered if I would recognize you if I happened to see you like that. And I did! It was an amazing feeling, but even more amazing to have you sitting across from me right now. Are you hungry? I'm sure you're hungry." He flagged down the waitress, who came by and took my order of iced tea and a turkey club. For the next fifteen minutes or so I did my best to fill him in on my life, telling him about Sean, how we met while volunteering at Taft Elementary, and about my cleaning arrangement at East Point Prep. It was like catching up with an old friend, the way he listened attentively and laughed or cringed at all the right moments.

Then he told me about his other children. Ben, the oldest, was in college. Olivia was a senior in high school and Zach was a year younger than me. He confessed that he hadn't told them about me yet, but that he would when the time was right, after the shock and anger over his divorce from their mother had worn off. Although I was curious about them, how they looked and what their personalities were like, the thought of meeting them in person was a little terrifying. I assumed that they would hate me, and would surely blame me for the dissolution of their parents' marriage, even though Greg insisted it had nothing to do with me or my mother. "Our divorce had been in the cards for years," he said. "Shelly hadn't been happy in a long time. I wasn't always a good husband, as you obviously know, and there was a lot that she resented me for, things like spending too much time at work and not enough time with the family, for expecting her to be the parent on duty all the time, not giving her more opportunities to take time for herself. She doesn't even know about my affair with your mother."

"If she had known would she have left you then?" I asked.

He sat quietly for a moment, rubbing his thumbs along his coffee mug. "I don't know," he said. "I thought that she might, but I knew that either way she would be really hurt, and I didn't want to put our family through that."

It was a strange thought, knowing how much pain my exis-tence could possibly cause another person who I'd never met. It was a reality that I hadn't fully grasped before, or that maybe I just hadn't let myself accept. To Shelly, my birth would have meant pain, a betrayal by someone she loved and depended on. I felt my face turn hot, recognizing that my birth hadn't been celebrated by both of my parents, that one of my parents was concealing it, hampered by shame and guilt. But then I remem-bered what my mom had said, about never doubting that she wanted me. Maybe it didn't really matter what Shelly would have thought about me then or now. I was my mother's daughter, and Shelly didn't have anything to do with that.

"Was it hard to keep me a secret from her?" I asked finally.

"It was the hardest thing I've done."

...

Mom came back an hour later, as promised. Greg stood outside with me and waved to her as she pulled up in front of the café. She smiled and waved back. "I'll call you later," she said to him as I got into the passenger seat. I realized then, as I looked back and forth between the two of them, that my mom had parted her hair differently, more to one side instead of directly down the middle, and that she'd traded in the baggy, cowl-neck sweater for a more form-fitting turtleneck. She looked lovely, and I was sure Greg had noticed.

"How was it?" she asked, beaming with elation.

"It was good," I said. "I think I'm still in shock."

"Do you want to tell me about it?"

I paused, trying to figure out how to best explain the experience. "It was an emotional rollercoaster. I find it so odd that his siblings and ex-wife don't even know about me. He says he's going to tell them soon, once the dust settles, but I can't expect them to take it very well."

"I wouldn't worry about that. I'm sure Greg will ease them into the situation. Let's just cross that bridge when we get to it." she said, putting her hand on my knee.

I wasn't convinced it wasn't worth worrying about, but I nodded in agreement anyway, trying to push the thought of a potentially disastrous meeting with my siblings out of my mind. I didn't want to dwell on the negatives when there was still a lot to be excited about. "He told me about his legal practice. I'm so relieved that he isn't the kind of lawyer who helps rich people get away with screwing people over. He actually helps the people who deserve it." According to my dad, he and his partner started out by taking on a big real estate developer who'd been intimidating property owners into selling their buildings for below market value, and then used discrimination in their rental policies. They'd won that case, and had done 'fairly well,' ever since. I didn't know what fairly well meant, but figured he'd been able to provide for his family without any problems.

My mom smiled. "I always knew he'd be good at what he does. It's practically impossible to win an argument against that man. That's why I didn't bother objecting when he told me that he's going to pay your school tuition from here on out."

"Wait, what?" I clutched at my chest, thinking I must have misheard or misunderstood.

"Your dad, I mean Greg, is going to start paying for school, effective immediately. We discussed it on the phone earlier, but like I said, I didn't object. He really wants to help us out financially, and I'm going to let him. He even wanted to pay me back for the last two and half-years, but I said no to that, since I didn't actually pay for much. You did, by cleaning. But now you don't have to. Now you can volunteer, or just have more time to yourself. Whatever it is you want to do."

"For real? This isn't a prank, right?"

"When have you known me to pull pranks?"

"Um, never."

Mom didn't respond right away, but put her arm around my shoulder and pulled me toward her. "You deserve this," she said after a moment. "We both do."

I nodded, but had no words. Everything that I'd ever wanted was finally within reach, and it was happening so fast that I could hardly process it. "I just can't believe this is really happening."

Mom laughed. "I honestly couldn't believe it at first either, but now that the shock has worn off, I am willing to accept any and all help Greg wants to provide."

"So, you're ok with him being this involved with us now?" I asked.

She let out a heavy sigh. "Yes, because I know this isn't something he takes lightly. He wouldn't have gotten in touch if he wasn't going to be in it for the long haul."

I thought back on all the times I'd been asked about my dad, and had to explain that he wasn't in the picture. But now he was very much in the picture, and as grateful as I was, I didn't know if I was quite ready for everything else that was going to come along with him. A burst of laughter escaped my mouth as tears started streaming down my cheeks.

"Are those happy tears?" Mom reached into her glove box and handed me a tissue.

"Yeah, I think so. I'm happy, just really overwhelmed."

Mom pulled into our driveway and shut off the car. As if she'd read my mind, she turned to face me and pulled me into a hug. "We're still us, Darcy. This isn't going to change who we are, ok?"

"Ok." I hugged her back, hoping to God that Greg wasn't going to let us down.

After we went inside, I went into my room and threw myself onto my bed. I grabbed my phone from my black shoulder bag and started to call Sean but stopped myself. I knew he would be excited to hear the news about my dad, but for some reason I didn't feel ready to share it. I needed more time to process it, to get a handle on my emotions before attempting to explain them to anyone else.

I put my phone down on my bed and instead opened up my notebook, which had been sitting on my nightstand. Maybe journaling about all that had happened over the last day would provide some mental clarity.

I just met my dad for the first time since I was a baby. I couldn't believe it when my mom told me that he wanted to see me. The weirdest part was that he'd already seen me before, and knew right away who I was. I never believed in fate, but it seems like more than coincidence that he saw me that night, because he's coming back into my life right at the perfect time. Still, I feel a little uneasy about it. It's a little like I'm jumping into the ocean, exploring the coral reef and seeing all the amazing colors and creatures, but knowing that there could be sharks lurking nearby. Greg is going to start paying for my school, which is amazing, but he has three other kids. How are they going to feel about this?

The sound of my phone ringing pulled me out of my thoughts. I didn't recognize the number on the screen, but I answered anyway, thinking it might be Greg. "Hello," I said.

"Darcy?" said the caller, and I knew right away whose voice it was.

"Ms. Rose?" I asked. My heart rate quickened as I went through all of the reasons a teacher would call a student during winter break. None of them could be good.

"Yes, it's me. I normally wouldn't call a student over break like this, but I have some important news. Is this a good time?"

"Yes, it's a great time," I said. I had no idea whether the news was bad or good, but I hoped conveying positivity would increase the chances of good.

"Great! So, I just wanted to let you know that I really liked your essay, and it got me thinking that maybe we could find a way to allow you to keep gardening and working with kids without giving up your tuition discount."

"Oh," I said, a bit baffled at how such a situation could be arranged.

"I hope you don't mind, but I let Mrs. Masterson read your essay. I explained to her how great you were with the kids and how much you'd learned, and she was really impressed with the whole gardening program concept and how much the younger kids benefited from it. So, we discussed it for a while and came up with a plan."

"Ok!" I said, springing up from a mostly horizontal position. I listened as Ms. Rose described her conversation with Mrs. Masterson regarding my tuition discount. Apparently, Mrs. Masterson had wanted to create some sort of outreach program for a while. Like Ms. Rose, she recognized the privilege of the East Point Prep students, and thought everyone could benefit from sharing the school's resources with the community surrounding it. So, Ms. Rose and Mrs. Masterson crafted a plan to start East Point's own urban gardening program that would serve elementary students from the nearby public school, which had demographics similar to that of Taft Elementary.

There was plenty of space on the school grounds for a garden, and a small fund set aside for landscaping that could be used to get the garden started.

"Here's where you come in," said Ms. Rose. "Instead of staying after school to clean every day, you'll stay after school to work in the garden and help the children who come from Mt. Washington Elementary. We'll recruit another student to help, but you'll be the one leading the program. You'll also have the Mt. Washington After School Coordinator there, so you won't be left without an adult to help manage the children. And since there won't be any gardening during the winter months, you'll use that time to plan and raise money for the upcoming gardening season. How does all this sound to you?"

I sat back down on my bed, knowing I needed to respond but unable to speak, as if the wind had been knocked out of me.

"Darcy, are you still there?" asked Ms. Rose.

"Yes!" I finally shouted. "Sorry, I was frozen there for a minute. I'm just so surprised, but I love the idea. I think it's amazing! Do you really think I can do it, though? I just don't want to disappoint anyone."

"Darcy, I believe in you," said Ms. Rose. "And you're not alone in this. I know I'm no gardening expert, but I'll do whatever I can to help. In fact, I'm going to make myself the official staff supervisor on this project. Luckily, Mr. Brooks will have plenty of advice for me."

"That's a relief," I said with a sigh. I knew that with Ms. Rose's help, my new duties would be far less daunting. "I'm going to start planning right away. I'll make a list of all the supplies we'll need, find out what it's going to cost to get started, and then come up with ideas for raising money."

"That's perfect. We'll touch base again after New Year's, ok?"

"Ok," I said, sensing that the phone call was winding down. "Ms. Rose?"

"Yes, Darcy?"

"Thank you so much for doing this. I mean, you've really gone out of your way to help me this year, and it's made such a big difference for me."

"You're welcome, Darcy. I'm happy to do it. Truly."

We both said our goodbyes and hung up the phone. "Was that Ms. Rose on the phone," said my mom, poking her head into my room. "I wasn't eavesdropping intentionally. I was just putting some groceries away in the kitchen and couldn't help overhearing a little."

"It's ok, Mom, and yes, it was. As it turns out, I don't need Greg to pay my tuition. The terms of my tuition discount are changing, so I'm going to keep gardening and working with kids, right at East Point Prep."

My mom ran to me and wrapped her arms around my neck. "Darcy, that's wonderful news."

For a moment we sat there, just holding each other, sharing in the mutual feelings of relief and happiness the day's events had produced. "Thank you for sending me to East Point, Mom. I haven't always liked it, but I finally feel like it's where I belong."

"They're lucky to have you there." She squeezed me tight before getting up and walking toward the door. "Let's go out to celebrate tonight. Do you want to invite Sean and Paige? Tell them it's my treat."

"Can Maya come too" I asked.

"Of course! I didn't know that the two of you had made up."

"Yeah, we finally worked things out."

"I'm glad to hear that." She smiled and headed back to the kitchen.

I closed my notebook and picked up my phone, this time clicking Sean's name and letting the call go through. I hadn't been ready to tell anyone about Greg, but I couldn't wait another minute to share the news from Ms. Rose.

TWENTY

A knock at the door pulled Mom out of the kitchen, oven mitt still on her hand. She opened the door for Greg, who walked in with a paper grocery bag in one arm and a large canvas tote in the other. "It smells wonderful in here," he said. He leaned down and kissed Mom on the cheek before walking into the kitchen and setting his bags on the countertop. Once his arms were free, he walked into the dining room and gave me a hug. I kept my arms at my side as I leaned into him, resting my head against his shoulder. It felt surprisingly natural, like a hug I'd received thousands of times before.

"You've done a nice job with the table decorations," he said.

"Thanks. I made the centerpiece this afternoon. I think it's one of my best creative achievements." I'd taken the branches that

Mom had to trim from the bottom of our Christmas tree and layered them around a tall white candle, adding on some pinecones and holly that we had in the yard.

"Should we light the candle?" asked Greg.

"Yes, we should." I grabbed the matchbox from the drawer in the China cabinet.

Greg lit the candle, then looked back into the kitchen, where Mom was frantically pulling items out of the oven. "Why don't you sit down, Julia? I can take care of the rest."

Mom looked uncertain, but Greg put his arms on her shoulders and gently guided her toward the table. She sat down next to me, and the two of us watched as Greg carved the turkey and pulled a baguette wrapped in foil from one of his bags. After he brought all the food to the table, he opened a bottle of wine that he'd brought and poured two glasses. "Is Darcy allowed to try this?" he asked from the kitchen.

I looked at Mom with pleading eyes. "Maybe half a glass, but only because you're at home being supervised by your parents," she said.

Greg poured what seemed like a shot of wine into a third glass, then brought all three to the table. "Thanks," I said, stopping myself from saying *Dad*. It still seemed too early to call him that, but he was starting to fill the role, and I could see myself getting used to it.

...

After eating dinner and two types of pie, Greg and I cleared the table and started with the dishes. When all the food was put away and the dishwasher was full, we went into the living room to open gifts. Mom and I each had something for Greg, but mom had already said that she wanted to save her gift for last, so I gave him mine first. I barely knew Greg at that point and didn't know what kind of hobbies or interests he had, but I knew that if he was a lawyer, he had to like reading, so I went out on a limb and picked out a book for him that I thought he would like and hoped he didn't already have.

"I've heard of this," he said, once he'd removed the wrapping paper from the copy of *Furious Hours* by Casey Cep. "It sounds fascinating. I can't wait to start it. Thank you, Darcy."

I breathed a sigh of relief and sat down on the couch. "You're welcome. I'm glad you haven't read it yet."

Then he handed me a box wrapped in shiny red paper with a white bow. I opened it to find a collection of brightly colored bohemian bracelets. They weren't something I would have picked out for myself. I hardly ever wore jewelry, but I still found them beautiful. "Thank you, Greg. I love them."

"The proceeds go to a nonprofit that supports women entrepreneurs in developing countries, which I thought you might appreciate," he said.

"I do! That's amazing." I slid on one of the bracelets, admiring the multi-colored strands. I had to admit to myself that they would look nice with a black dress, if I wanted to get dressed up for New Year's.

"This one's for you, Julia." Greg handed Mom a larger item wrapped the same way.

She tore the paper and pulled out a long, burgundy coat. She gasped as she held it out in front of her. "It's gorgeous," she said. She put it on over her jeans and sweater and twirled around in it, giving Greg and I the full three-sixty view.

"It looks amazing on you, Mom."

"Perfect for a night out on the town," said Greg.

"I can't wait to wear it out!" Mom buttoned the coat and tied the sash. It was the first time I'd seen her in a coat that didn't look like it was made for skiing, which was ironic because I don't think she'd ever gone skiing in her life.

"How about New Years?" asked Greg. "I haven't made reservations or anything yet, but I bet I can find something fun for us to do."

"I would love that," said Mom. She and Greg both looked at me.

"How about you, Darcy?" asked Greg after a beat.

"Oh, I've already made plans. Paige is picking me up and then we're both going to Sean's house. You two should still go out, though!" Greg and Mom smiled at one another. I had a feeling that they weren't disappointed about the prospect of a night to themselves.

"Greg and I do have a lot of catching up to do." Mom bent down to pick up a present from under the tree and handed it to Greg. "And I think this will help with that."

"Is that right?" asked Greg. He ripped off the wrapping paper to reveal a leather photo album. Mom sat down on the other side of him and watched as he began flipping through the pages. She had spent the entire day in her room getting his present ready, and now I understood why it had taken so long. The album was filled with photos of my childhood. My first ice cream cone, first day of preschool, my proud pose next to the sand turtle I'd made on the beach in Florida, all moments Greg had missed out on.

Mom pointed to the photos and explained where and when everything was taken. Greg nodded and wiped tears from his eyes. I didn't know if it was that he didn't want to say anything, or if he was just too emotional to talk, but watching him get choked up made me cry too. I wiped the tears away at first, but after the first few just let them fall. I didn't know if we were crying over a sense of sadness that he had missed out on all of those moments or if it was happiness that he was finally seeing them. He put his arm around my shoulder and squeezed tight before letting me go. The little girl in the photos was fine without her dad, and I was still fine without him, but I was glad he was there.

...

"Open mine first," I said to Sean. It was Christmas day, and he'd come over to exchange gifts with me.

His eyes nearly popped out of his head when he tore the wrapping paper and saw what was in the box. "These are the best pencils you can get," he said. "These are perfect, just what I need. I hope you didn't spend all your money on them, though. I know they aren't cheap."

I shrugged, a satisfied smile spreading across my face. "I made pretty good money from my babysitting jobs."

"Well, my gift to you is very apropos, I think," said Sean, handing me a large gift bag with tissue paper popping out.

"It's heavy," I said, grabbing a hold of the handle. I set down the bag and pulled out a framed picture. It was a drawing that he'd done of me, one that I hadn't seen before. In this one I appeared to be brushing loose strands of hair out of my eyes with most of it pulled back into a loose bun. My facial expression was sultry, one I would probably try to use if I were walking a runway, but didn't think I'd ever actually pull off. "This is beautiful, Sean. I love it! Do I ever really look like that?"

"Yeah, sometimes. When I close my eyes and imagine your face, that's how I see you."

"It's incredible. You're incredible. Thank you." I leaned into him and put my arms around his neck. He looked back at me with a comforting smile. I studied his face for a moment, wanting to make sure I could always think of him this way when closing my eyes. I leaned in to kiss him, knowing he was always more shy to make a move at my house when Mom was home. But he kissed me back anyway, gripping my waist as he did.

We separated when we heard the sound of Mom's footsteps approaching the living room. She came in holding a tray of mugs filled with hot chocolate and a plate of decorated sugar cookies that we'd made the day before.

"Thank you, Ms. Walsh," said Sean, picking up one of the mugs.

"It's too warm outside for hot chocolate," I said.

"I know," said my mom with a sigh. "But we can't break from Christmas tradition."

"Ok, you've twisted my arm enough." I took a mug and a snowflake cookie. My mom set the tray down on the coffee table and went back to the kitchen. We still had leftover pie from the night before, but she'd insisted that she needed to bake fresh ones to bring to my grandparents' house that night for our Christmas dinner.

Sean and I finished our hot chocolate, then went outside for a walk. Ever since talking to Ms. Rose the week before, I'd had a knot in my stomach that I couldn't seem to work out. As exciting as it was to know that my time as the school cleaner had come to an end, I couldn't help but worry that I wouldn't be able to handle running a gardening program on my own. One of the reasons I'd become so confident while volunteering for Taft was because I knew I'd have Sean there for support, but Sean wouldn't be at East Point, and I still had no idea who I would recruit for help. "Do you think I'm going to be able to pull it off?" I asked.

"Pull what off? The gardening program?"

I nodded and sighed, attempting to release my anxiety. Sean grabbed my hand and brought it up to his mouth, kissing my fingers lightly. "Of course you will. And I'll help, as much as I'm permitted to."

"Do you think you can help build the raised beds? I have no idea what I'm doing when it comes to using tools, and I don't think either of my parents have much other than a couple hammers and tape measurers."

"I can get that done. I'll make Tyler help us too. His dad is a pretty good carpenter, so he knows a lot and has all the tools we'll need."

Hearing him say 'we' released some of the tension in my stomach. It reminded me I wasn't alone in getting this program off the ground. "That would be amazing! Tell him I'll buy him all the chicken tikka masala he can eat if he helps me. Seriously, it would be tremendous if he could borrow his dad's tools."

"Trust me, he won't want to miss out on showing off his muscles to all the girls at your school. All you have to say is girls and he's there. But I'll take the tikka masala."

"I'll treat you both. I may just need to pick up a couple more babysitting jobs."

Sean put his arm around me, pulling me in toward him as we walked past the house with the giant, inflatable Santa Claus. "You know, as much as I'm going to miss being with you at Taft, I think it's really cool that your principal is starting this program. I can already tell how much happier you are."

"Yeah, I do feel pretty happy right now. And none of this would be happening if it wasn't for you, Sean."

Sean chuckled. "I mean, I know I am pretty great, but I don't think I can take credit for this, Darcy."

"You taught me so much at Taft. I wouldn't have a clue how to do this if it weren't for you."

"I think you'd have figured it out on your own, but I'm still glad I got to help you out."

After our walk Sean went back to his house for his annual family Christmas gathering and I changed into a fuzzy cream sweater and black jeans in preparation for dinner at my grandparents' house. I found a hammer and a nail from the drawer in the kitchen and hung Sean's drawing above the dresser in my room. It felt strange to display a portrait of myself so prominently, but it was beautiful, and it was a gift from Sean. He was the one I would think about whenever I saw it. He always would be.

...

On New Year's Eve Paige came over to my house with every dress she owned. I laughed when I opened the front door to see them cascading from her arms. "Have you ever worn the same dress twice?" I asked as she entered my room and dropped them onto my bed.

"Nope, and neither has my mom. She gives her used ones to me, so I have double the selection."

"You could seriously open your own boutique." I spread out the dresses and ran my fingers along their fabric. A black one caught my eye. "Didn't you wear this to homecoming last year?" I asked, holding it up to my chest. It was knee-length with a row of fringe along the front, like a 1920s flapper dress.

"Oh yeah. I love that dress. You should totally wear it tonight. I think I'm wearing this." She said, holding up a champagne-colored slip dress.

"Wow. That dress will be practically lethal on you."

"You think so? My mom does have pretty good taste. And she still has the body of a twenty-year-old."

"Wear it! I can't wait to see how many guys pass out at the sight of you."

Paige rolled her eyes. "I'm going into your bathroom to change."

We finished changing and walked out into the living room at the same time as Mom, who was getting ready for her date with Greg. She was wearing a form-fitting, black dress with long, lacy sleeves.

"You girls look incredible!" she said.

"So do you, Ms. Walsh."

"Well, it's not every night an old lady like me goes out on the town. This is probably my one and only chance to get dressed up for the year."

I had a feeling that this was only the first of many dates with Greg, but I kept that to myself. Whatever was going on between them, whether it was friendship or something more, I didn't want to make it about me. I didn't want to pressure Mom or Greg to be anything other than my parents, or maybe I just didn't want to jinx the possibility of them finally having a chance to be together. "Have fun tonight, Mom," I said as I hugged her goodbye. "Don't wait up for me. I'll probably be home late."

"Just make sure to let me know if you two need a ride. Absolutely no driving if you've had anything to drink."

"We promise," said Paige.

Mom kissed me on the cheek and Paige and I walked outside. The days had been warm but the nights were still cold, and we shivered in our thin cardigans that covered the tops of our sleeveless dresses. "Maybe we should have worn coats," I said as we rushed to get inside of Paige's car.

"The heat will kick on after a minute." Paige started the car and turned on the headlights. "Ok, now tell me where I'm going."

I directed her to Sean's house, taking the most direct route. Right onto Edwards Road, past the shopping center, left on Wasson, and right on Paxton. When we pulled onto Sean's street, there was already a long row of cars parked along the curb leading to his house. We found a spot several houses away from his, and practically ran in our heels to get out of the cold.

"Hello, Darcy! Come in. Come in," said Sean's mom as she opened the door for us. She radiated glamor and beauty in a red cocktail dress with her hair pulled back in a French twist. The party was already in full-swing. The kitchen was crowded with friends of Sean's parents, many of whom were hovering around the vast spread of hors d'oeuvres on the countertop. Sean's dad was leaning against the bar, locked in conversation with two other men. Lively jazz music boomed from the wireless speakers in each room. I waved a bit, then brought Paige into the basement, where the teenagers were congregating.

"Damn! Look at you," said Sean as we descended the steps. He stood up from the couch and strode toward me, then grabbed my hand and pulled over toward the couch, where Tyler, Tess and a few of their other friends were sitting.

"I hope we're not overdressed," said Paige. Everyone else in the room was in jeans or stretchy pants.

"Hell no!" shouted Sean. "It's New Year's Eve and you both look amazing. We're playing Deplora-cards. Come join us."

Paige and I squeezed in at the end of the couch, and watched as they finished the round. It was a guy named Avi's turn to hold the black card, which stated: *Protesters in California rally against* _____. After a moment of deliberation, the results from the other players came in. Dog farts, crippling debt, topless sunbathing, Disney princesses, and insurance deductibles. Avi chose *dog farts* as the winner—a girl named Madison's card.

"Hmmm, I would've gone with Disney princesses," said Paige.

"Thanks, Paige. That was my card," said Sean.

"But that's something people in California might actually protest, so it's not as funny," said Tyler.

"It is funny, because it's just far enough outside the realm of plausibility, but still kind of makes sense. Protesting dog farts doesn't make sense," said Paige

"Which is why it's funny," said Tyler.

"I guess we just have to agree to disagree," said Paige with a sigh.

"I'm with you, Paige," said Sean, reaching over me to give her high-five.

"Me too," I said, patting her on the back. "I think princesses was the funniest."

"Thanks, Darce," said Sean. He leaned in and kissed me on the cheek.

"Aww," said Tyler. "You guys are the epitome of cute couple. I have to say, Sean, it's making me a little jealous."

I laughed. "Sure, Tyler," I said, even though I believed he might have meant it. Much like Tristan, he had a reputation for dating around, never committing to just one girl for more than a few weeks. But unlike with Tristan, I saw in Tyler an ability to dedicate his time, his passion and his whole self into an art form that he loved, often spending days memorizing lines, weeks perfecting his delivery and pouring every ounce of his energy into becoming whatever character he was taking on. Although, maybe it was his love of drama that made all the breakups inevitable. Still, I thought that he might be good boyfriend material, if he found someone that could rein him in a little. Even though he wasn't anything like either of Paige's previous boyfriends, I saw a potential match in the two of them, and hoped that they could hit it off, at least for one night. But after the princess card disagreement, I wasn't so sure my match-making scheme would go according to plan.

We continued playing the game, laughing and arguing about which responses were best. More of Sean's friends trickled in. After less than an hour, the basement was bordering on crowded, with some people playing pool in one corner of the room and singing karaoke from a portable machine that someone had brought along in the other corner.

As our card game winded down, Sean leaned in and whispered into my ear. "Since neither of us is driving anywhere tonight, do you want some champagne?"

I hesitated. I'd never actually tried champagne before, and wasn't sure if I'd like it or if I wanted to experience another hangover. "Do you think you can even get any?" I asked.

"I'll go try," he said, getting up to head upstairs.

I sat between between Paige and Tyler. Paige was looking around the room, twirling a lock of her hair around her finger and Tyler was tapping his foot against the floor. I knew what I had to do. "I'm going to the bathroom," I said to Paige.

The basement had a bathroom opposite the stairs, so I didn't have to go far. I spent a few minutes touching up my eyeliner and pinning back the fly away hairs on the side of my head. When I came out, Paige and Tyler were sitting closer together, and talking, just as I'd hoped. I sat back down next to Paige and pretended to read something important on my phone as I listened to what Paige was telling him about East Point Prep, how we'd recently become best friends, and about how much she liked Sean and me as a couple. "I think they helped me realize that I wasn't really happy in my own relationship, so I broke up with my boyfriend a few weeks ago."

"Oh," said Tyler. "And how do you like being single?"

"It's nice. I guess I miss having a boyfriend sometimes, like right now for example. It would be nice to have someone to kiss at midnight, but I'd rather it be someone I'm really into than someone I'm just going through the motions with."

"Right on. I couldn't agree more," said Tyler.

Sean came back down the stairs, two half-full champagne flutes in his hands. "You don't know what kind of obstacles I had to go through to get these. I'm like Odysseus tonight."

"Does that make me Penelope?" I asked, taking one of the champagne flutes from him. "It did feel like you were gone for like ten years, but I stayed faithful."

"Damn. How'd I get such a smart girlfriend?" said Sean, handing me one of the glasses.

"Is it midnight already?" asked Paige.

Sean checked his watch. "It's 11:58."

Someone turned on the TV. "We don't have cable," said Sean. "Only Netflix and Hulu."

Everyone began pulling out their phones to find coverage of the ball dropping in New York. After a moment it seemed almost everyone had it pulled up in front of them, just in time for the countdown. "10, 9, 8, 7. . ."

I looked away from the phone to see Sean's face. He was smiling, beaming really, and I couldn't believe how perfect everything was. For my whole life, I'd convinced myself that this feeling was unattainable, and now here it was. But how long would it last?

"3, 2, 1." Sean turned his head to look at me and gave me a kiss. It was slow and soft, like a first kiss. It was our first kiss of the year. We picked up our champagne glasses and clinked them together.

I took a small sip and turned to Paige, who was pulling herself away from Tyler. I didn't see it happen, but I knew she'd kissed him. "Happy New Year," I said to them.

"Happy New Year," shouted Tyler, pumping his fist in the air.

"I have a feeling it's going to be a great year," said Paige.

I imagined all that was to come: a new job at East Point, something meaningful I could take responsibility for, a chance to connect with more kids, more opportunities to bond with Greg, more memories with Sean—my first love. Maybe this year, I would tell him how I felt. I had to agree with Paige. 2020 was looking very promising, but maybe it was all too good to be true.

The End

Afterword

Dear Reader,

Thank you so much for picking up this book and taking a chance on a new author. This story is the product of many years of drafting, revising, and editing, and is very loosely based on some of my own high school experiences. Darcy, however, is much better at handling the trials and tribulations than I was.

If you want to continue Darcy's story, be on the lookout for *From a Distance*, the sequel to *Cleaned Out*. Feel free to visit www.PaddisonPress.com for updates on the release of this book, as well as new writing projects.

Cheers,
Suzanne

ABOUT THE AUTHOR

Suzanne Williams has been reading and writing stories for most of her life. She lives in Cincinnati with her husband and three daughters. *Cleaned Out* is her first novel. She plans to follow it up with many more.

Printed in Great Britain
by Amazon